LOVE NOTES

WITH THE BAND
BOOK TWO

TANYA RENEE

Serenade Publishing

Serenade Publishing

www.serenadepublishing.com

To all of those perfectly imperfect people who struggle and fight their silent battles. You are not alone.

ALSO BY TANYA RENEE

Primrose Series

Prairie Sky

Prairie Nights

Prairie Fire

Prairie Hearts

Prairie Sound

Prairie Rain

With The Band

Finding Direction

Love Notes

On The Edge Of Forever

Steve stood at the edge of the stage, feeling butterflies take flight in his belly as he looked out at the crowd in the auditorium. He glanced up at his mother, her smile radiant and proud as she beamed down on him and gently squeezed his hand. Crouching down, she leveled him with her kind gaze, her blue eyes so bright and beautiful like the color of a cloudless sky.

"I know you're nervous, Stevie, but I promise you that you're going to be just fine. Just look out at the crowd before you play, and you'll see Daddy there watching you from the front row, okay? Try to imagine you're just at home, playing for us like you do every day." She suggested with a reassuring stroke of her hand across his cheek as she turned to face the stage. Steve's eyes followed her eye line to the shiny grand piano in the middle of the stage. "And do you see that big, beautiful piano? You get to play that. You get to sit on that bench and make something beautiful for everyone in the audience to hear."

Steve surveyed the large black grand piano curiously.

With its lacquered finish that reflected the stage lights, he wondered if he could see his reflection on its surface. What would the keys feel like under his fingers? It was like the big pianos on the videos he would watch of great concert pianists entertaining in huge concert halls. He was curious about what it sounded like. Was it loud? Was it clear? *I want to play that piano.*

"Okay, Mommy," he said, reflecting her encouraging smile.

A master of ceremonies took the stage and stepped to the microphone. "Next up we have the ages five to eight category. First up is seven-year-old Steven Furgallo, playing the jazz piece "Dream a Little Dream of Me" on the Piano."

"Okay, baby, it's time. I'll be right here, and remember Daddy is in the front row watching." His mother reminded him with a nervous smile.

Steve swallowed down his nervousness, turned and his eyes zoned in on the beautiful ivory keys across the stage. Walking out onto the stage, the lights were blinding, but he paid them no mind, his entire focus on the magnificent grand piano he was approaching. Slipping onto the bench, Steve turned his head and glanced down at the sea of faces watching him, spotting his father immediately, his eyes shining and smile wide. He gave him a thumbs-up. Steve turned to the keys, his hands itching to play. Setting his hands in place, he closed his eyes, taking a brief moment to feel the smoothness of the ivories under his fingers as he heard the song in his head, the notes writing themselves on the sheet music in his mind. Hitting the first note, the clear, crisp sound from the piano, making his eyes fly open and widen as his hands glided over the keys with ease. He imagined he was like those concert pianists he watched, and the entire auditorium grew silent as he played. He wanted to play more than one song, stay here for hours discovering what this piano could do; however, his rogue thoughts were interrupted as he ended the song and the auditorium erupted with applause, everyone rising to their feet. Glancing over at his father, who was clapping proudly, his face wet with tears, Steve's brows furrowed. *Why is he crying?* Sliding off the bench, he stood facing the crowd as his mother coached him to do and bent to take a bow. The applause swelled as he turned, rushing off the stage into his mother's waiting arms.

"Stevie, that was beautiful." His mother cooed, kissing both of his cheeks, making him squirm and giggle. "Did you see all those people out there? They loved it too. We are so proud of you, Stevie."

She wrapped her arms around him in a hug, and the familiar warm and safe feeling he always got in her arms enveloped his body and made his nose tingle.

"Excuse me," a woman said, abruptly breaking their embrace as she stood with her hands on her hips, glaring at them both. A little girl beside her, close in age to Steve, stood by her side, hands on her hips too, mimicking her mother.

"I'm sorry, we'll get out of your way," his mother said as she got to her feet and reached for Steve's hand.

Steve's eyes locked on the stare of the little girl who was dressed in a pretty yellow dress, with a wide hooped skirt that made it look like she was floating on air. She had a bright yellow bow in her dark brown ringlet hair, and her dark brown eyes were the color of a night sky. She looked like a real-life princess in one of his sister's movies, and Steve's gaze transfixed on the little girl with wonder. He had never seen anyone more beautiful or angelic, and as they passed, his lips tilted up into a friendly smile. The girl squinted at him, then scrunched up her nose and stuck out her tongue, making him frown. *That wasn't nice.*

"Next up is seven-year-old Emersyn Bridger singing Beauty and the Beast."

Despite her less than kind greeting, Steve's eyes widened as he watched the little girl go onto the stage, with a confidence well beyond her years. *Beauty and the Beast is Raya's favorite movie.* Tugging on his mother's hand, she looked down at him curiously. "Mommy, can I watch her?" he asked, pointing towards the stage as the pretty little girl got to the microphone.

"Sure, Stevie." she replied, and they turned around to watch, his mother as enraptured by the little girl on stage as he was. The intro music started, and when the little girl opened her mouth to sing the first note, his mother put her hand to her heart as the little girl's voice, sweet and angelic, soared through the auditorium. Steve closed his eyes, taking in every rise and fall of her sweet voice, pure and perfect. A confusing mix of feelings stirred in his chest as he listened intently, not wanting to miss a single note. Listening to the little girl made him happy yet made him want to cry in equal measure.

"Your daughter sings beautifully." His mother complimented, sincerity in her tone.

The girl's mother turned to face his mother, eyed his mother up and down speculatively and answered, "Looks like my daughter is giving your son some competition," with a tone that Steve unmistakably knew wasn't nice. Steve's eyes darted up to his mother. The look on her face both baffled and disappointed. His mother wasn't one for conflict of any sort, her heart too kind to be a pot stirrer, so she simply offered the girl's mother a hesitant smile and glanced down at Steve, saying, "Let's go find daddy."

Steve nodded, taking her hand just as the pretty princess in the yellow dress took her bow on stage.

CHAPTER 1

A core memory is one that stays with you and is part of your internal makeup. Part of the intricately woven fabric of your soul. It is something you come back to again and again, and it fills you with emotion, sometimes good, sometimes bad. Luckily for Steve Furgallo, most of his core memories were good, and although the bad ones did hover on the edge of his consciousness from time to time, now at 28, they seldom made themselves known.

One of his earliest core memories was the day he and his two-year-old sister, Raya, went to live with their adoptive parents, Antonio and Dahlia Furgallo. Although he was young, he remembered that day so distinctly. He was four years old, being brought to a pretty blue house with white shutters and an overhang that covered a bright sunshine yellow front door. Two people stood at the door, who he now knew as his parents. They were tall, good-looking and sharply dressed. Just like it was yesterday, he remembered his father's button-down shirt that was the same color as the house and his mother's long golden blonde hair, which he thought looked like strings of pure gold. Their eyes were kind, and their smiles so bright and welcoming. His sister Raya, who was scared, started crying as she clung to the social worker, and he remembered telling her it was okay because these people would take care of them and love them. Raya, with her eyes filled with fearful tears, gave him the most trusting look and, with hiccupped breaths, she went willingly into their new mother's arms. He remembered glancing up at his mother and seeing her lashes flutter rapidly as tears trailed down her cheeks, which he wanted to touch and wipe away with his hand as he wondered why she was crying and if he could fix it.

Part of the core memory that always stood out to him was the how safe he felt, like he was finally home and would finally know what it was like to be loved. And he was loved. He and his sister grew up with so much love in their house, he almost felt guilty for those that didn't have what they had. They were given opportunities that many would have only dreamed of. His parents embraced him, and his sister and they were never made to feel like a second choice to them, with his adoptive parents unable to have children of their own. He and his sister lived a truly good and privileged life, and if it weren't for that life, he never would have found music.

As a child, curiosity was something Steve had in spades. He always wanted to touch, feel, and see everything. He was quiet by nature but would ask questions when something fascinated him, and from the day he walked into his new home; he was fascinated by the piano standing tall in the corner of the living room. An old upright Mason & Risch piano, with a deep dark wood finish and weathered keys the color of antique ivory. He loved to sit on the long wooden bench and play each key, listening to the sound it would make and thinking about what each sound compared to. Even before he came to live with his parents, he would hear sounds everywhere. He heard pitch, tone and beat. His ability to hear these things, so much a part of him that he wasn't even aware that maybe he was different from other kids his age and could be considered gifted.

It wasn't until he was watching a TV show with his parents, all of them snuggled up on the couch, that he felt the uncontrollable need to sit at the piano and mimic the song he was hearing on the TV screen. Hearing each note so clearly, he climbed up on the bench, pressed a few keys just to match the tone, then started to play the song. He remembered his mother's gasp of surprise as she held her hand to her mouth and his father rising from the couch to stand by the piano and watch him, disbelief and wonder in his eyes. He wasn't sure what all the fuss was about at the time as he heard the song and simply wanted to play it, but as he continued to play, he could see the pride on his parent's faces, and he knew he was special. He was five years old.

As a declared wunderkind, and with his parents wanting to share his talent with others, he willingly competed in talent competitions and festivals. For the most part he enjoyed it, but as he got older and his musical interests matured, he preferred something with more of an edge, looking up to incredible musicians like

Geddy Lee, Freddy Mercury and John Paul Jones. He loved how the music they played and the lyrics combined to make pure magic, so he aspired to be just like them.

Looking back at how his love for music began, he was proud of what he did with his natural talent. As the official composer and keyboardist for a popular indie rock band, Prairie Sound, being a member of the band gave him endless room for creativity and the chance to play the music he loved most. Luckily, his parents supported him, although he was sure they had grandiose dreams of seeing him play in classical auditoriums rather than in dingy bars and later, concert venues. Either way, they were proud of him, and he was living his dream.

Steve pulled his long black hair back, twisting it into a makeshift man bun as he stared down at the lyrics his bandmate Layne put in front of him. He could already see the notes forming in his mind as he hummed the tune to himself. It was a Saturday afternoon and he, along with his bandmates Ramiro Perez, the lead singer and Layne Stark, the bass guitarist had plans to pick away at a few new song ideas and run through all the songs they had for their second album, set to drop this coming summer. Steve looked around the new studio Rami had designed for them on the grounds of the new home he shared with his wife Savanah. The studio was modest and similar in size to the Layne's garage, where they practiced for over a decade. The only difference was their new space had everything state-of-the art, decked out with all the equipment they could ever want or need. Although he loved the new space, sometimes he missed the nostalgic comfort of the cold, dingy garage.

On top of a new studio, the past four years had brought a whirlwind of changes for their humble garage band. The first was the seemingly overnight viral success of Prairie Sound. All it took was a few videos going viral to help open the door of opportunity and ride the wave of success to where they were today. It had been quite the ride too. A platinum debut album, two major tours with big names like Aerosmith and the Rolling Stones, and this fall they would be embarking on their first national tour across Canada with them as the headliner. First things first, they needed to decide which songs they were going to record and finish their second album in the studio.

As for other changes, there were plenty. Rami and Savanah had been married for two years and had bought a beautiful property at the end of Main Street, Primrose. Layne reunited with his high school girlfriend, who had emigrated from Germany and was now a proud Canadian citizen. Layne was a dad, with he and his wife Juli welcoming a baby girl, Tabitha, a few months after they were married. Rex, their drummer and probably his best friend in the whole world, hadn't changed much. He was still the same womanizing, foul-mouthed, drinks too much guy he always was, and yet that was part of his overall charm.

"Have either of you heard from Rex?" Steve asked, checking his phone to see if there were any missed messages.

"I haven't." Layne replied. "But I haven't been out of

the house much lately. Tabs has decided sleeping is for chumps, and poor Juli has been running herself ragged for *Entertainment Weekly*. I've been on full nighttime dad duty," he said as a yawn escaped.

Steve smiled. It was fun to see his long-time friend as a dad, and Layne was a great one.

"He hasn't messaged me either. I did speak to him a few days ago, and he said he would be here, but have any of you noticed how he has been a no-show a lot lately?" Rami asked. "I mean, Rex has always been late for practice, but it's hit or miss if he'll even show up these days. I haven't said anything as he always shows up to gigs, but something is going on with him." Rami and Layne turned to face Steve. "You're closest to him, got any ideas as to what's going on with him?"

Steve sighed and gave them an uneasy look. "Honestly, I think he's been drinking a lot again. I mean, he's cleaned up his act before, but it seems that he's off the wagon again," he answered. "You know Rex, he starts, he stops, he starts, he stops. He has done that with alcohol and weed for years. It's sort of his pattern."

They both nodded, knowing full well what Steve was talking about. Just then the door of the studio flew open, and Rex appeared, his blue mohawk now slicked back and his indigo eyes red-rimmed and glassy.

"Fucking sorry, guys. Had a late-night rendezvous with Charlene and, well, let's just say the party for two ended an hour ago, if you know what I mean." he said waggling his eyebrows at them as he took a seat behind his drum set, picked up his sticks and hit the cymbals.

The guys were very familiar with Charlene, a busty

redhead Rex had been seeing on and off for the past year. She was well known for sinking her long fingernails into any local bad boy, and she instantly had her sights on Rex. Not that Rex was all that bad. Yes, he swore far too much, yes; he had a reputation for bedding more women than most and yes; he drank like a fish and enjoyed the odd joint, but he was from a good family in St. Augustine and was very well connected. Rex had a strong work ethic instilled in him at an early age working for his father's trucking company, and although he was chronically late, when he was there, he worked hard, and he always brought something amazing to the table. That's probably why they let him off so easily.

"Please leave the details at the door, Rex," Layne said, rolling his eyes as he picked up his guitar and turned to Steve. "Okay, maestro, what are you hearing?"

Steve glanced at Rex, knowing he needed to table a conversation with his friend, offered Layne a smile and started to play the tune in his head.

* * *

STEVE WALKED into the Everything you Knead bakery in Primrose and took a deep inhale of the comforting smell of fresh baking in the air as he stepped to the front counter. *Damn, it smells good in here.*

Marnie Baxter, Rami's sister, came flying out of the back kitchen with a large pan of freshly made Danishes in hand. "Steve!" Marnie greeted as she spotted him. Marnie was the self-proclaimed big sister to everyone in the band, whether you had siblings or not. She was funny and sweet but also a total badass when she needed to be. Seeing that she married a burly redheaded military man seemed fitting, and Steve adored her. She slid the pan into the showcase and turned back to him, meeting his eyes with a question, "What brings you to my bakery?"

"I'm here to meet up with Dee Jones," he said, glancing at the freshly baked Danishes. "But now, I think I'm here to try one of those."

Marnie let out a laugh and cocked an eyebrow at him. "I can do you one better, Steve, and plate you up two. Besides, you are far too skinny, and I know how big your appetite is," she said, looking up at him and giving him a wink.

Marnie had made it her mission to feed him every chance she got. He was tall, six foot two, and had always had a slim, lanky build. The truth was, he couldn't gain weight if he tried and always had a ravenous appetite, the joke being that the food went straight to his size fourteen feet. His opinion was, if Marnie was going to feed him, he was going to eat it.

The bell of the bakery door chimed, and Marnie and Steve's heads turned as Devine Jones stepped inside. Lowering her sunglasses, Dee oozed cool, rocking retro wide-leg jeans, a bright green sweater, and her signature black rocker-style jacket. Her crochet braids were wrapped up at the top of her head with a multi-colored scarf, and Steve's eyes feasted on the gorgeous woman before him. Steve had to admit he had been harboring a bit of a crush on Dee since he met her. It was hard not to. Dee Jones was the definition of a sexy, confident woman, and any man would be lucky to have her on his arm.

Sadly, despite all attempts to the contrary, he was friend-zoned upon meeting her and had stayed in that zone ever since.

"Hey there, String Bean," she said, sidling in next to him and giving him a playful nudge.

"Hey, Short Stuff," he countered, putting his arm around her for a friendly side hug, as she wrapped her arm around his waist with a reciprocating tight squeeze.

Marnie plated the danishes and poured them coffee as they settled into one of the tables by the large windows overlooking Main Street Primrose.

Steve leaned back in his seat and surveyed Dee, his eyes twinkling with amusement as he said, "I'm super curious why you wanted to talk to me today. Unless of course this is a date, and this is your way of getting me alone without Rex."

Dee shook her head, rolled her eyes, and let out a huge guffaw. "That guy is relentless, and sorry to tell you, Steve, but you're not exactly my type. Far too handsome and sweet for your own good, but not what I'm into," she added, giving him a shrug as she picked up her coffee and took a sip, her midnight eyes danced playfully.

Steve threw his head back with laughter at their banter and shrugged. "Hey, had to shoot my shot." he replied resolutely as he trained his eyes on her and asked. "Seriously though, what's up?"

Dee put her coffee down and leaned forward, her elbows on the table, meeting his inquiring gaze. "As you know, I'm the new drama teacher at Primrose High, and every year we do a spring musical." He nodded, having heard Savanah talk about her new job. "And this year being my first year, I'm going to take on an ambitious one."

"Okay, how can I help?" he asked, leaning forward to mirror her with genuine interest.

"Well, we're going to do *Singin' in the Rain,* and from what Rami tells me, you're a bit of a savant on the piano. Like, you could be a concert pianist, kind of good," she said. "Soo... I was wondering if you would consider volunteering your time to be the pianist for the production. It would involve a lot of practices, working alongside the vocal coach, and you would of course need to be there for all the performances as well as the dress rehearsal."

Steve winced and leaned back against his seat, letting out a long exhale as he replied, "That's a huge commitment, Dee, and with everything that Prairie Sound is working on right now. Finishing up the songs for the new album and preparing for the tour this Fall, I'm not sure I should be taking on something like that right now."

Dee flashed him her megawatt smile and reached for his hands, her big, beautiful eyes pleading for him to agree. "It's only a few months out of your life and I know it's a lot, Steve, but I would be forever grateful if you said yes." She let go of his hands, flashed him a confident dimpled smirk as she picked up her coffee, leaning back against her seat and added, "You know I still haven't cashed in that favor you promised me."

Steve chortled and shook his head. "You're good, Dee. Damn you." He really did owe Dee a debt of gratitude. She had been instrumental in orchestrating Prairie Sound's big break, filming the videos that ultimately went viral and working with them initially to manage their social media. Without her expertise and push, they may not be where they were today.

He looked down at his long fingers, the fingers he knew could make magic on the piano if they wanted to, and sighed. *She has you backed into a corner.* Looking up, meeting her expectant gaze, he conceded, "Alright, Dee, I'll do it."

Dee's face brightened as she popped up from her chair and enveloped Steve in a grateful hug. "You are the best!"

Steve laughed and returned her hug as he asked, "So who is the vocal coach I'm going to be working with?"

"A friend of mine from my theatre days." Dee replied, taking her seat again, her face beaming with excitement. "She's an incredible singer, super talented and an amazing vocal coach. Her name is Emersyn Bridger."

Emersyn Bridger. Steve's stomach instantly sank as he repeated her name in his head, and he immediately regretted agreeing to this.

CHAPTER 2

*E*mersyn walked into Primrose High School, shook the rain off her ringlet curls and cursed herself for not bringing an umbrella. She glanced from side to side, seeing only a few staff members and students in the hallway. *Class must be in session.* Seeing an open door right next to the entrance, she peeked around the corner to find the school office. The school secretary, Mrs. Cartwright, looked up from her computer, her glasses on the bridge of her nose as her face brightened in welcome.

"You must be Ms. Bridger!" she exclaimed, rising from her seat, and putting her hand out to Emersyn. "Dee told us you'd be coming by today. We're all very excited for this year's musical and thank you for lending your expertise. I think you're going to be shocked by the talent in our little school."

"We will see," she said, feigning the friendly secretary a smile and reluctantly accepting her hand. "Can you direct me to the auditorium?"

Mrs. Cartwright laughed, her perfectly coiffed silver hair bouncing with her chortle. "My dear, if you mean our gymnasium, it's just down the hall, and you will see double doors with the sign 'gym' above it. You'll find Dee in there with her students."

Emersyn nodded and made her way down the hall with furrowed brows, passing rows of lockers and closed classroom doors. *No auditorium. What have I gotten myself into?* Her longtime friend Dee Jones was freakishly persuasive, and she caved. *Oh, well, it's only two months out of my life.* Besides, she was in between productions and needed a distraction right now, the bonus being time with her dear friend.

Finding the gymnasium as directed, Emersyn entered and frowned with distaste upon seeing the wide-open space and cinderblock walls, wondering how the acoustics were going to work for such an ambitious project.

"Emersyn!" Dee exclaimed, running over to wrap her in a tight hug. Dee Jones was the epitome of happy, positive energy, and you couldn't help but smile in her presence. *Exactly what you need right now.*

"Hi Dee," she greeted as she leaned in and whispered. "What have you roped me into here?"

Dee put her hands on her hips, cocked her head and gave her a chiding look, knowing her friend was ever the pessimist and perfectionist. "Em, you promised me you would be open-minded."

Emersyn rolled her eyes at her friend's accurate presumption of her mood and shook her head conceding. "Yes, yes. I know I promised."

"Let me introduce you to the rest of my production team and my cast. They're eager to start learning the songs." She said, guiding her over to a wide-eyed group of students.

Scrutinizing the cast of students as Dee made introductions, they turned, and she took her over to Oliver Boyce, an incredible choreographer whom she knew very well from the musical theatre community.

"Oliver, Dee wrangled you into this as well?" She asked honestly, surprised that someone of his caliber would want to do a small production like this.

Oliver flashed her an affirming smile, gave her an amicable hug and planted two kisses, one on each cheek. Holding her out at arm's length, he answered with a dramatic sigh, "You know, Dee, she always gets what she wants. Besides, I'm excited to do something small for a change, teach some young aspiring thespians how to dance like Gene Kelly." Oliver did a little tap step routine, and the students turned at the sound, watching with awed expressions on their faces.

"Show off." Dee scolded cheekily as she led Emersyn towards the piano. "And this is our pianist extraordinaire and bona fide rockstar, Steve Furgallo."

Dee stepped to the side as Steve rose from the piano bench, stepping forward to join them.

Emersyn's eyes looked all the way up, and she had to pick her jaw up off the floor as they met the most gorgeous dark onyx eyes she had ever seen. Eyes she knew far too well. There before her was the boy she competed against in more competitions than she could count, but gone was the timid young boy, who was replaced by a proud and confident man. A very tall man, who towered over her petite stature, well over six feet she estimated, slim and lean in build with broad shoulders and a rich tanned complexion. His handsome features were dark, and a dusting of facial hair kissed across his strong jaw, giving him a hint of an edge that both unnerved and intrigued her. He had long black silky hair that he had pulled back in a hipster man bun, which she had to admit looked super sexy on him. *Did I just refer to Steve Furgallo, my past nemesis, as sexy?* She shook her head, trying to erase the distracting thought, and looked up at him, completely shocked to see him here after all these years. Trying to school her thoughts, she raised her chin to meet his waiting gaze as she put out her hand and said, "Hello, Steve, pleasure to see you again."

Dee's eyes widened in surprise as they darted back and forth between them asking, "You two know each other?"

"We used to compete against each other at festivals and talent competitions when we were kids." Steve answered, indignation in his tone, his dark eyes piercing hers.

His voice was rich and smooth, a deep timbre that made her heart flutter a little. *Seriously, Emersyn, this is not like you. Get yourself together.* She feigned Steve a saccharine sweet smile and turned to Dee and Oliver, both watching with amused interest. "Steve and I go way back."

Dee clapped her hands together excitedly as she exclaimed, "Good! Then you will be an amazing partnership! You will be working closely together throughout production."

Emersyn glanced up at Steve, reading the displeasure

on his handsome face and looking like he wanted to be anywhere but standing in front of her at this moment. Her stomach bottomed out as the harsh realization of that vexed her to her core.

* * *

STEVE TOOK his seat at the piano as Dee organized the kids and brought the pretty blonde girl, who was playing the Kathy Selden character in the play, over to Emersyn, introducing her. Emersyn glanced at Steve and gave him a nod as if cueing him to play. Laughing internally, he sat there, hands on his lap, a smile tugging at his lips. She nodded again towards him, with no detailed directions passing between them. *If they are supposed to be a team, someone was going to have to learn how to communicate properly.* Turning towards him, she put her hand on her hip, frustration on her face as she informed, her tone dripping with condemnation, "A nod is your cue to start playing, Steve."

Steve cleared his throat, cocked his head slightly and flashed her a smile. A smile to kill her with kindness. "I realize that Emersyn, however you didn't say what song you wanted me to play. I may be able to play the piano without sheet music, but I don't read minds."

Emersyn let out a little huffed breath, loosened her stance and brought her plump bottom lip between her teeth. That tiny gesture, going straight to his groin. *What the?* His body's reaction shocked him as he met her obsidian gaze, now showing glimmers of sheepishness, but still holding onto her fierce pride as she asked in a steady voice, "Could you play "All I Do Is Dream of You", please?"

Softening his gaze, he nodded his acknowledgement of her request. Mirroring him, she pivoted to the student, giving her a sweet smile as she asked her to sing. As he played, he glanced up to watch Emersyn, this time able to take her in fully. *She is gorgeous.* Her piercing midnight eyes framed with impossibly long dark lashes, full pink lips in the perfect pout and a lush head of long rich brown hair in enviable ringlets. She was petite, maybe five foot two if that, and had a delectable curvy figure he found incredibly sexy. Emersyn Bridger had transformed from that pretty little girl in a yellow dress to a sassy pre-teen, his last memory of her to a remarkably stunning woman, and he as a hot-blooded man couldn't help but notice. *If only she had a personality to match the beauty on the outside.* Instantly feeling guilty for thinking it he groaned internally as he glanced to his fingers floating over the keys. It was mean and out of his character to think such a thing.

The truth was, Steve had a massive crush on Emersyn when he was a preteen barely old enough to understand what a crush was. She had always been beautiful, paraded around by her overbearing, managing mother from competition to competition. Her mother was well known for bullying and bad-mouthing anyone that might get in the way of her perfect daughter winning a competition and, unfortunately, her mother had her sights on Steve and his family. Having overheard the conversations and the words she used to describe their eclectic family; he had heard himself be referred to as "that strange, adopted boy" more times than he could count. After five years of competing, his parents ultimately decided to pull him out of the competitions, and he was certain Emersyn's mother was a contributing factor in the decision. Besides, he had grown tired of the competitive atmosphere and was growing up, wanting to play his music, his way.

Stealing glances at Emersyn, he was surprised at how encouraging she was to the aspiring ingénue. Not what he was expecting considering what he knew about her. She gave the student tips and walked her through any vocal challenges with patience, and when they were done, he couldn't help but ask himself, *Is she just a product of her upbringing?*

* * *

EMERSYN HAD to admit she was impressed with Dee's casting for this production. Her students were eager, all had wonderful voices and by the end of the practice, she was certain this cast was going to knock this musical out of the park.

Dee approached Emersyn and put her arm around her waist giving her a half hug squeeze. "How did it go?"

"Really good. You have some naturals here." She complimented, reciprocating Dee's affectionate embrace.

Dee nodded her head, obvious pride on her face as she continued curiously. "How did it go with Steve? I felt some weird tension there that I'm not going to lie, sort of surprised me." she said, glancing over to Steve who had gone rogue on the piano, playing "Singin' in the Rain". "Steve is probably the calmest, coolest guy I've ever met, and I've never seen him angry or frustrated. I have never seen him glare at anyone the way he glared at you."

Emersyn glanced over and scrunched up her nose, internally cringing. "Some stuff may have gone down, back in my competition days. My mom, you know how she is."

Dee let out a huff of breath and nodded her head, knowing full well the wrath that was her mother. Constance Bridger was a force to be reckoned with and Emersyn was the apple of her eye. She put the stage in stage mom and was determined to make her daughter a star, stomping on anyone that tried to get in her way. Having worked with Emersyn on several productions, Dee had experienced her mother's brand of nastiness before and didn't wish it on anyone.

"How is Mama Bridger these days?" Dee asked, her brows drawn together.

"As good as can be expected. She's slipping away more and more. What she does remember about me is usually from my younger years. They say it's normal to have flashbacks of the past. It's just hard to deal with some-times." Emersyn answered, meeting Dee's inquiring gaze. "She gets agitated sometimes and reacts, sometimes lashing out. It's not fun."

Dee nodded, empathy in her eyes and gave her another hug as Oliver pirouetted over to join them. Oli never stopped dancing and his expertise and passion for the arts was a part of his undeniable charm. His presence instantly lifted the mood, as they laughed at their dear friend, and Emersyn shook her head as she asked, "How was your practice?"

"Pretty good." he replied, with a bright smile. "You've got some super talented students." Dee beamed proudly again as Oliver leaned in, eyes flitting between the two ladies. "Tell me more about that tall drink of water at the piano. Seriously, the man is knock me on my ass good looking without even realizing he is, if you know what I mean?"

Dee chuckled and glanced at Steve who had now transitioned to what she recognized as a Billy Joel song and had starstruck students gathered around the piano.

"He's a good-looking guy for sure." Dee agreed, looking at Steve fondly. "And literally the sweetest guy as well. He's actually in that rock band, Prairie Sound, you know the one whose lead singer married my best friend, Savanah Smithfield, or I guess Perez now."

Oliver nodded and gave an admiring glance to Steve and Emersyn followed his gaze, taking Steve in as he entertained the students. *Steve's in a rock band?*

"Why would he decide to play in a rock band?" Emersyn asked curiously. "Steve could have literally been a concert pianist. He is a virtuoso when it comes to music and plays everything by ear."

"Seriously?" Dee asked. "Like no sheet music?"

"I'll bet he didn't use it right now during vocal practice." Emersyn said looking over at him, a smile tugging at her lips.

"Wow." Oliver said with a dreamy look in his brown eyes and a playful wiggle of his brows. "Drop dead gorgeous and talented."

That he is. One of a kind.

<h1 style="text-align:center">CHAPTER 3</h1>

It had been a very long day, and all Steve wanted to do was eat his pizza and watch some mindless TV. Pulling out his phone, he dropped the pizza box onto his coffee table, lifted open the box and grabbed a slice, taking a satisfying first bite. Sinking into his couch, he swiped open his phone to check his messages. 3 texts.

Rex Johnson: *Where the fuck are you, man? Going out tonight. Charlene has a friend for you to meet. You need to get laid, my friend.*

He let out a big guffaw and shook his head. Not a chance was he going to take that bait. Rex may be his best friend, but hanging out with Charlene and her friends wasn't his scene. Glancing back at his phone he clicked on the second text.

Dee Jones: *Thank you so much for coming out today. You're amazing as always!*

Steve smiled; *today was surprisingly fun.* He looked back down at his phone and clicked on the last text. A name he was not expecting popped onto his screen and he had to do a double take. *Emersyn Bridger.* "How the hell did she get my number?" he said aloud. Curiosity building, he clicked on the message which read:

Emersyn Bridger: *Steve, Dee gave me your number. I guess because we need to coordinate. Not sure I understand why. Here's my number if you need it, although I don't think it's necessary to call me.*

Steve shook his head, not surprised in the least by the tone of her text. Setting down his phone on the coffee table, he reached for the remote, flipping the TV on as his thoughts went to Emersyn. On the outside Emersyn appeared to still be the same stuck-up pretentious girl she was when they were kids. Still icy and demanding. Yet he couldn't help but think that maybe there was more to her than what was on the surface. He saw glimmers of kindness as she worked with the students. Perhaps he needed to get to know her again before he passed his judgement.

* * *

WALKING INTO GRANDVILLE RETIREMENT HOME, Emersyn's heart instantly sank. Despite the home being welcoming and charming, with warm brick walls, comfortable visiting areas, and friendly staff, as nice as this place was, she hated that her mother, at only 54 years old, had been reduced to living in a place like this. She was still young and would be vibrant if it weren't for her terrible disease.

She approached the front desk, giving the young nurse there a half smile as she signed in as a guest. The nurse mirrored her wary smile with one of her own as she informed, "Your mom has been asking for you, today."

Emersyn gave her a hesitant smile, nodded and walked down the long corridor, trying to face forward, not wanting to see any of the other residents, sadly alone in their open-door rooms. She hated coming here, seeing so many people simply sitting alone, many with no family to visit them. It made her sad and seemed to punctuate her situation. With her mother sick, her father long erased from the picture and no known relatives, she was very much alone in the world. Having never known her father, the story being that he left them when she was just a toddler, she never had anyone but her mother. She didn't have grandparents that she knew of and no aunts and uncles with her mother being an only child. Now with her mother slowly losing her memories, she was more alone than ever, and that loneliness felt like a dark looming cloud over her life.

Rounding the corner, she stopped at her mother's door, taking in a deep calming breath, and letting it out slowly, trying to mentally prepare herself for whatever scenario awaited her in her mother's room. The door was closed so she knocked lightly and opened it slowly. Her mother was sitting by the window quietly, watching the branches sway in the spring wind, as rain pelted the windowpane in a steady staccato rhythm. A constricting lump of emotion formed in her throat, but she swallowed it down as she approached her mother slowly.

"Hey, Mom." Emersyn greeted, her voice soft and tentative.

Her mother didn't turn, just continued to stare out the window, an unreadable look on her face.

So, that's how it's going to play out today? Emersyn took a seat next to her in a second chair. Her mother, having been in this facility for six months, was still not thrilled by her daughter's decision to put her in the home. The truth was, with her Alzheimer's taking over and her condition in a moderate state she needed more than homecare could provide. She needed to have 24-hour care and Emersyn was lucky to have gotten her into a facility this nice and as quickly as she was able to.

Her mother turned to her, her brows furrowed, her lips pursed tightly into a thin line. "I hate it here and I hate you for putting me here. There are too many old people, and this room is atrocious." She said, her Caribbean accent thick and searing as her eyes darted around the room. Bringing her piercing gaze back to Emersyn she squinted as she spoke low between her gritted teeth. "You just wanted my money. To sell our house and take all the money."

Here we go again. Emersyn shook her head and rolled her eyes. This was a conversation they revisited frequently, and it exhausted her. She went into her usual monologue. "Mom, you, and I both know that you were unable to take care of yourself, and this place has the best possible care for you. It came highly recommended by your doctor. And you know too, I sold the house so I can pay for this care as this is a private facility. All your money is in a special account you agreed upon and there to pay for your accommodations in this facility and to provide you with quality care. I make my own money and can support myself."

"My doctor is an idiot." She growled in frustration letting out a huff of breath.

"I know Mom." Emersyn replied, leaning in, reaching for her hand and giving it an affectionate squeeze.

A faint smile tugged at her mother's lips as she stared down at their joined hands for a moment, and she turned her gaze to the window again. Watching as the rain picked up it started hitting the windowpane harder, the steady beat it created oddly calming. *Got to love spring in Manitoba.* Emersyn turned looking out the window too. *Mom really does have a nice view of the gardens, and it will be beautiful once the spring flowers started to bloom.* Emersyn was grateful for this place. Grateful that her mother's sole care wasn't her own anymore. Grateful that she could have a life again. She considered that for a moment, through their collective silence. *What are you doing with your life and this newfound freedom?*

Not having been on a date in years, and at 27, she should be out there, meeting guys, going on dates, and having... Emersyn halted her thoughts. The idea of intimacy with another person, almost scary at this point. Having been so long since her last sexual encounter that she wasn't even sure what she liked anymore. All of her sexual experience was wrapped into three years, from 18 to 21, or as she liked to call them, her rebellious phase. Having been raised by a mother who loved to control everything in her life, and who paraded her around like she was a show pony, as a teen she was determined to break her mother's hold on her and do what she wanted. So, when she turned 18, legal age to make her own decisions she went wild. That included dating and getting herself into situations she wasn't proud of. She cringed just thinking about some of the things she did back in those days. Actions of a young woman who had been held back from living her life all in the name of perfection. It wasn't until her mother was diagnosed with Alzheimer's that she cleaned up her act and put her exploration into adulthood on the backburner.

Her mother suddenly turned to her, and she met her gaze offering her a smile. Enjoying this unexpected quiet moment with her mother. Then before Emersyn could register what was happening her mother's eyes went from present and bright to cloudy and she rose to her feet in front of her, raised her hand and slapped Emersyn across the face with the back of her hand, saying "I told you to hold that note! The judges want to see everything you can do! Why don't you listen to me? Don't you want to be the best?" she said with anger and contempt dripping from her words.

Shocked, Emersyn held her cheek, feeling the heat of her contact under her palm as she pushed back her chair, scraping it across the floor, scrambled to her feet and pressed the call button for the nurse.

"I told you that Bridgers always win!" her mother shouted her hands fisted at her sides. "Don't you want to win?"

An orderly and a nurse ran into the room, her mother now shaking with agitation and pacing in front of the window. The nurse glanced at Emersyn, giving her a compassionate look, and put her hand on her shoulder. "I think it's better if you end your visit now. We'll calm her down. Are you okay?"

Emersyn nodded still in shock at what just happened. It wasn't the first time her mother had done this, and she was sure it wouldn't be the last. It was painful though. Both physically and emotionally. Like reliving all the bad memories from her childhood, she wished she could erase. Hot tears pricked her eyes as she grabbed her purse and rushed out of her mother's room, wishing this wasn't her life.

ANOTHER PRACTICE and Steve had to brace himself for another afternoon with Emersyn. Entering the gymnasium, he saw Emersyn and Oliver in a heated discussion with a man about Steve's age, blonde hair, wide broad build, like a professional wrestler, dressed in gym clothes. Confused, he approached not sure what was going on and glanced around quickly searching for Dee. As he approached, he caught their conversation.

"We have every right to be here. We have practice today and this space has been approved for our use." Oliver said, his arms folded over his chest and his brows furrowed tightly.

Emersyn flagged him, trying to look tough but looking more apprehensive with this muscle-bound man looming over them.

"What's going on?" Steve asked, stepping in line with Oliver and crossing his arms as well. "Do we have a problem here?"

The guy looked up at him and let out a smug guffaw as he scoffed, "What a waste of time." His eyes flitted from Steve to Oliver then drifted languidly over to Emersyn. An arrogant smile curled his lips as he looked her up and down and flashed her an arrogant wink, then walked away.

An unexpected protectiveness tightened in Steve's chest as he turned to Emersyn then Oliver. "Are you guys, okay? Who is that jerk?"

"The gym teacher, Anders." Emersyn replied with a combination of disgust and apprehension in her tone as she added. "Dee warned me he may try to cause problems, but he's insane."

Oliver looked up at Steve and met his concerned gaze, "When I got here, Anders was all up in Emersyn's space."

"He was hitting on me, and when I told him to back off, he blew up about us using his space." Emersyn replied, shaking her head. "You got here at the right time, Oli."

Steve gritted his teeth and glared towards Anders who was lingering around his office door, looking like a world class douche. "Did he touch you?" Steve asked, bile rising in his throat.

Emersyn shook her head, looking at him with a somewhat bewildered look on her face. Obviously not expecting Steve to be so bothered by the whole situation. A smile crept up Oliver's face as he surveyed his agitation and batted his eyelashes, hooking his arm through Steve's. "What about me? Will you protect me if I need it, Steve?"

The tension in Steve's shoulders loosened as he met Oliver's questioning gaze and let out a chuckle, "If you need my protection, sure of course."

Oliver offered him his megawatt smile, let go of Steve's arm and turned to Emersyn as he said, "Look at that Em, we have our very own, hot, rockstar bodyguard. Seriously Steve, Dee was right. You're a gem." he said, tossing him an air kiss as Dee entered the gym from her classroom with her cast following behind. "Time to mold my dancers!" Oliver sang out as he pirouetted and bowed, then strode toward his side of the gymnasium.

Emersyn laughed, needing the surge of endorphins to ease the tension. "Oli is a character." She said as she watched him go, a huge smile on her face. She turned looking up at Steve with gratitude and sincerity in her voice. "I appreciate the backup with Anders."

Steve's dark gaze locked on hers as he replied, "Any time." Emersyn's eyes softened with his words as she studied him, an ember of heat reflected in her midnight stare. Suddenly realizing she was staring, she cleared her throat, dashed her eyes away and fidgeted with her music stand, seemingly uncomfortable. *Interesting.*

She fluttered her hand to shoo him towards the piano and gave him an annoyed glance, "Are you playing for us today, or just standing there?"

A smile curled his lips and Steve shook his head as he took a seat at the piano bench and let out a chuckle. *There she is.*

IT HAD BEEN A LONG TIRING day in the studio and Steve was grateful for the text from his mother, to come over. He rolled up to the blue house with white shutters, and the yellow door, the only one like it in their cul-de-sac. Every time he drove up, that distinct core memory hit him along with the feeling of love and security from that day. He loved his childhood home.

Striding up to the front door, he entered, knowing he was never expected to knock. "Mom, Dad!" he shouted from the front entrance.

His mom came around the corner, a dish towel slung over her shoulder and her golden hair twisted up into a knot at the top of her head. Dahlia Furgallo was a social worker by day and wannabe chef by night. Her kitchen was her refuge from the heaviness of her career and whatever she was cooking right now made his stomach growl in appreciation. "Hey there Stevie." she said, pulling him in for a hug. "I haven't seen you in a few weeks and I missed that handsome face."

Smiling down at his mother whom he towered over by about five inches, he leaned down and kissed her forehead with affection. Steve felt that familiar adoration in her presence, his mother's heart as big as the sun. Wrapping her arm around his waist she gave him an affectionate squeeze, her eyes shining with happy tears. His mother was emotional, especially when it came to her kids and her heart was worn permanently on her sleeve.

They walked into the open area living space and his dad was at the stove stirring something in a large pot. Inhaling deeply, he smiled, feeling instantly comforted by the familiar smell wafting from the kitchen. *Mom's amazing Beef Stew, my favorite.*

"Steve, my boy." his father greeted, setting down the spoon and coming over to give him a hug. His father was a tall man, the same height as him, with dark salt and pepper hair and kind blue eyes. Although Antonio Furgallo was unquestionably Hollywood handsome, he settled for a job as an engineer for the city of St. Augustine. "Raya's in the living room." he said, gesturing over to the couch where his sister sat.

Steve turned to see his younger sister Raya, completely focused on a reality TV show about aspiring fashion designers. She was slouched into the cushions, her legs stretched out and feet crossed at the ankles as they rested on the coffee table. Steve climbed over her legs; her eyes not leaving her show.

"Hey there Dork." she said, elbowing him as he settled in next to her.

"Dweeb." he replied, nudging her back.

She grinned and turned to meet his eyes. Her dark eyes softened as she surveyed him then turned back to her show, tucking her long straight black hair behind her ear. He and his sister had a close bond despite their banter to the contrary. Many times, he considered how lucky they were to have been adopted together when they were younger and to haven't been split apart and put into the foster care system. Their lives could have taken very different trajectories if that were the case, but thankfully, he would never have to imagine what life would be like without her.

"Dinner's ready!" their mother sang out as she set the steaming cast-iron pot on the table and their father set down a basket of fresh bread and Bannock.

They gathered around the table, each taking their designated seats, and joined hands as they always did, bowing their heads in prayer. As an adult Steve wasn't sure where his beliefs stood on religion, but he respected his parent's devout traditions.

His mother ladled out bowls of the savory beef stew and handed them around until everyone including herself was served. "What have you been up to lately, Stevie?" his mother asked, passing around the basket of bread. "Working hard on the second album I assume?"

He nodded his mouth full of the delicious stew. He chewed, swallowed and replied, "We recorded a few singles today and have a few more studio sessions to complete it. It's going to be incredible for sure."

"I have no doubt." his father answered, proudly.

Steve smiled, his parents so incredibly proud of his music career and undoubtedly his biggest fans.

"Anything else going on? No girlfriends we need to know about?" his mother asked pointedly.

Steve laughed; his mother was always checking in on his love life. Although she never said it exactly, she worried about him. Wanting him to find love and experience all that a relationship like the one she and his father shared, had to offer.

"No, mom. No girlfriends. Dee Jones is still turning me down." he said feigning disappointment. His parents, having met Dee at their first album drop party, instantly adored her. "Alas, I couldn't charm her with my striking personality and undeniable good looks."

Raya almost choked on her food as she burst out in a fit of laughter and reached for her water.

He leaned over and punched her arm playfully, then added. "She has a boyfriend now." he said with a shrug, as he dipped a piece of Bannock into the gravy of the stew. "Nice guy and she seems really happy."

"Good for her." His mother said, watching him carefully. "I like Dee. You need someone with that kind of spunk. Someone that will get you out of your shell a bit more."

Steve leaned back in his chair, a little stupefied by his mother's comments. "Out of my shell? I get on a stage on a regular basis, Mom. How much more out of my shell do you want me to be?" he asked with an incredulous laugh.

"I know, I know." she acknowledged as her eyes trained on his. "You know exactly what I mean though, Stevie. You play music, you hang out with your bandmates, you go home, and you spend far too much time alone."

He conceded as his mother did have a point. But he liked the quiet sometimes, and it was his comfort zone. Besides, he had his piano and his music, so in his mind, that was all he needed. Seeing an opportunity to segway from his love life, or lack thereof, he said, "Speaking of Dee, she's putting on a production of *Singin' in the Rain* at Primrose High School and I'm playing piano for the production." His mother's face brightened as he went on. "You'll never believe who she has me working with." Everyone's eyes around the table lifted from their food to look at Steve as he revealed. "Emersyn Bridger."

Silence overwhelmed the table as everyone stilled, their eyes wide as Raya clarified, "Isn't that the daughter of that horrendous woman that would always try to take over all the music festivals. I was just a kid back then, but even I knew she was a piece of work."

"One and the same." Steve replied. "And Emersyn is as pretentious as ever. But she's a friend of Dee's, so I am trying to make nice."

His father shook his head, likely trying to dispel the memories of all those competitions. "I don't like to speak ill of anyone, but that woman was incorrigible."

Putting her spoon down, his mother clasped her hands together on the table and looked down at them, then slowly met Steve's gaze as she spoke. "You know, I always felt sorry for Emersyn. Her mother dragged her around from competition to competition, showing her off and honestly wasn't even nice to her. I remember so many times when I would hear her yell at her daughter telling her she didn't do her best and needed to do better. That's got to be hard for a young girl to hear all the time. You probably feel like you're never good enough and you carry that with you into adulthood. Always trying to achieve greatness and never giving yourself any grace. Have you ever considered that maybe, Emersyn comes across pretentious or hifalutin because that's her armor against the world."

Steve thought about his mother's words, her perceptions ringing true in his mind. *Was Emersyn the way she was as she never felt good enough? Was all her bossiness, sharpness, all those rough edges, her way of protecting herself?* His initial gut feeling that there was way more to Emersyn Bridger than what she showed to the world, hit him hard. *Maybe you need to put all your judgments aside and get to know her more so you can truly figure her out for yourself. Offer her some much-needed grace.*

The gym emptied; all the students let go for the day. Steve looked down at the keys of the school's baby grand piano, and a sense of nostalgia filled his chest. It wasn't exactly like the grand piano he would play when competing, but this was the closest he had come to since those days. Running his hands over the keys, he always loved the feel of ivory under his fingertips. Smiling, he thought of an Adele song he had heard on the radio on the way to Primrose and started to play it. He closed his eyes, feeling the notes as his fingers glided over the keys, the sweet sound of the piano filling the large space and taking him to another place. As he played, emotion rose, and a transcendent feeling washed over him. Playing piano had always done that to him. It made him feel alive and whole, like a part of him was missing without it.

His reverie was broken by the most beautiful voice he had ever heard, powerful, pure, and excruciatingly honest. Opening his eyes, Emersyn was leaning on the piano, singing, asking someone, perhaps him, perhaps the world, to go easy on her. Steve's eyes were transfixed, the once sweet angelic voice of a child, now full, rich and womanly, yet painfully vulnerable as she caressed the notes. There was an ache that edged her tone as she sang, as if the lyrics of the song held profound meaning. He couldn't look away. Steve almost felt like he was intruding on a private moment as Emersyn poured her heart and soul into the song. Pure magic escaped her lips. Playing the last note, he held it, not wanting this unexpected intimate moment between them to end. He met Emersyn's gaze, her eyes glistening with hopelessness, a melancholy expression on her face. Her midnight eyes betrayed her vulnerability. She took a deep breath and looked away, breaking their eye contact as she slipped on her jacket.

"I was wondering if you could walk me out. I don't trust the douche bag over there." She said, gesturing over to Anders, who was leaning against the wall next to his office door watching them.

"Yeah, of course." Steve replied, rising from the piano, pinning Anders with a narrowed glare and reaching for his jacket.

Walking out of the gym together, the school was all but empty except for a few staff lingering around in their classrooms. The silence between them was thick, Steve sensing she had something she wanted to say to him. They walked out of the school; the relentless rain of the season having turned into big snowflakes drifting soft as feathers from the sky. Emersyn stopped mid-stride, closed her eyes, and put out her tongue as flakes landed and instantly melted. They clung to her long eyelashes and ringlet hair, and for a moment Steve saw the little girl he had known all those years ago. The difference was this girl wasn't being dragged around backstage, being primped, and preened. For a moment he saw her as carefree, and it was mesmerizing.

Emersyn slowly opened her eyes and glanced up at him, as if waking from a dream. "Sorry, I love it when the snow falls like this," she explained softly. "It just makes you think anything is possible."

Beguiled by the moment and completely in awe of her beauty, Steve wanted nothing more than to pull her into him and hold her. Perhaps brush his lips to her mass of ringlet hair with affection. Tamping down the urge, he asked, "Where are you parked?"

She gestured over to a practical little hatchback parked next to his SUV. "That's me," she said, walking over.

"I'm right next to you." he smiled as they slowly strolled across the parking lot. "So next practice is on Tuesday?"

She nodded, and he turned to face his vehicle, clicking the unlock button of his door as she continued. "Dee asked me to find costumes and accessories for this production. Use some of my connections from the theatre world. The problem is I don't think I have enough room to transport them." She mentioned, glancing over to his big SUV and capturing her bottom lip with her teeth.

Steve leaned against his vehicle and asked with an inquiring smile, "Are you asking for my help, Emersyn?"

"Call me Em, and can you?" she asked, flashing him a sweet smile as she went on. "I know it's probably completely out of your way, but I don't know who else to..."

"Sure, anything you need." he interrupted, shocking even himself at how agreeable he was to spend time with Emersyn outside of practice, how much he liked the idea of calling her Em and how stunningly beautiful she was when she smiled. "Text me the time and place."

She nodded, fidgeting nervously with her car keys, and lingered awkwardly, as if she had more to say or didn't want their interaction to end. *Perhaps she doesn't want to go home?* The thought passed through his head as he surveyed her curiously, seeing his past nemesis through different eyes.

If he was being honest with himself, he didn't want it to end their interaction either. This was a side of Emersyn he had never seen, and he was intrigued. A thought drifted through his mind, and before he could second guess himself, he blurted out, "I don't know about you, but I could use an end of the week late afternoon pick me up. Have you been to the bakery here in town?" Her dark eyes flashed, and he could see by the expression on her face he had piqued her interest. "I know the owner, and she makes the most amazing desserts. After the long practice we had, I could use a little sugar therapy. Did you want to join me?"

Hesitating a moment, she glanced at her watch, making him think either she had somewhere to be later or was trying to make it look like she did. Meeting his inviting gaze and trying not to smile, she answered, "Ahh, sure, why not? Should I go with you?"

"Absolutely, hop in," he replied, clicking his key fob to open the passenger door.

Eagerly, she rounded his vehicle and opened the passenger side door, glancing at the seat that was otherwise occupied with sheet music he was working on.

"Sorry," he apologized as he quickly gathered up the sheet music and gestured for her to get in. She climbed in, and he stretched across the console to set the papers on the backseat. As he did, the sweet smell of coconut tickled his nose as he leaned closer to her with the reach. *God, she smells good.* Tempering the desire to lean in further and inhale her delicious scent, he sat back down, but not before catching Em watching him, her eyes zoning in on the exposed skin of his abdomen where his t-shirt lifted. Settling back into his seat, he straightened himself out and glanced at her, a playful smile tugging at the corner of her lips. *She just checked you out.*

EMERSYN LOOKED AWAY QUICKLY, glancing out the window, feeling heat creep up her face to settle in her cheeks. Swallowing down the dryness in her throat, Steve watched her curiously for a moment and let out a low, deep chuckle before starting his vehicle. He had caught her full out ogling the smooth caramel skin of his lean stomach, that seemed to go on forever. She had to internally stop herself from reaching over and touching the exposed skin to see how deliciously warm it would be under her fingertips. Another wave of heat hit her body, settling deep in her core and she fidgeted in her seat, knowing she needed to stop this train of thought. It was hard though. So hard to be around such an impossibly beautiful man and not drool profusely. It had been a month since she had started working with Steve and was finding herself warming to him in a way she had not expected. He carried himself with a quiet confidence and self-assuredness that she found incredibly sexy. Plus, as Dee had said he was truly the sweetest guy. *Am I crushing on Steve Furgallo?*

Turning onto Main Street, they passed the feed mill, hardware store as well as several other businesses before they pulled up to an adorable little bakery with a sign that said, "Everything you Knead." *Cute.*

They both got out of the SUV and Steve held open the door for Emersyn, a gentlemanly gesture she appreciated. Flashing him a grateful smile, she entered, immediately being overtaken by the most glorious decadent smells. She inhaled deeply, and her mouth started to water as she took in the quaint bakery. The bakery was bright and cozy, with a long countertop and showcase filled with decadent desserts. There were five tables of four along the large windows overlooking the main street, and all but one were occupied. Steve gestured to the empty table and took off his jacket, claiming it, with her following his lead. A gorgeous woman with dark brown curly hair and big, beautiful chocolate brown eyes came flying through the swinging door of the back kitchen, holding a tray of warm, fresh, gooey cinnamon buns.

"I know what I'm having." Steve said, rubbing his hands together and licking his lips.

"Steve! Let me guess, you smelled them a mile away, didn't you?" the beautiful woman said with a knowing laugh.

"It's Wednesday, of course, Cinnamon Bun Day! How are you, Marnie? I heard the good news. Congratulations!" Steve said, coming around the side of the counter to give her a hug. He planted an affectionate kiss on her head, and Emersyn was taken aback, his gesture so endearingly sweet.

The woman placed a hand over her barely noticeable belly and beamed with joy. "We are excited that Finny will have a sibling."

Steve must have caught Emersyn's inquiring gaze and realized he hadn't made introductions. "Emersyn, this is Marnie Baxter. She's the older sister of my bandmate, Rami Perez, and she owns this bakery."

Ah, that's the connection. "Hi Marnie, I'm Emersyn Bridger," she said with a smile as she put out her hand formally to Marnie.

Marnie wiped her hands on her apron, took her offered greeting and met Emersyn's eyes with a kind smile. "Nice to meet you. I heard you're the brilliant singer and vocal coach that's helping Dee with the spring musical. Dee and Jaxon were in here the other day, and she said, you guys are amazing together." She went on as she plated them each a large cinnamon bun smothered in cream cheese icing and turned to face them. Marnie looked down at the plates in her hand and laughed. "Sorry, I never asked if you wanted one."

Emersyn's stomach took that moment to growl audibly, and Emersyn laughed, placing her hand over her stomach. "I believe the answer is yes."

Each ordering herbal tea to go with the confection, they returned to the table they had claimed. Emersyn set the most decadent pastry she had ever seen in front of her and looked up at Steve, who was watching her intently. Glancing back down at the cinnamon bun again, she said, "How am I supposed to eat this, it's huge."

"Apparently the best way is to pick it up and just bite into it. It's going to be messy, but I heard that's the only way to tackle it," he said, picking up his cinnamon bun, ooey gooey brown sugar and butter dripping from the centre.

Squinting her eyes apprehensively, she glanced back down at the confection. Her mother would never have let her dive into a dessert like this. In fact, she probably wouldn't have let her even have this dessert at all. She would have given her a million reasons why sugar was bad for her. There was always a million reasons not to do something. *She's not here,* she reminded herself as she made the decision to dive in. Carefully, she picked up the cinnamon bun, following Steve's lead, and smiled at him as she asked, "Now what?"

"Now we bite it. Take a huge bite and get the icing all over our faces," he said playfully as he watched to see if she would do it.

"I don't know..." she started until he interrupted.

"When in Primrose, do as the Primrosians do, or something like that," he laughed. "Are you ready? On the count of three, 1, 2, 3..."

Emersyn wanted to be bad, and it smelled so good. Eyes locked on Steve's, she bit into the cinnamon bun just as Steve did, getting sticky, sugary icing on her nose and cheeks. The smell was just a tease as the incredible taste of spicy cinnamon, sweet brown sugar, rich butter and tender pastry hit her tongue in a symphony of flavors. The tangy sweetness of the cream cheese frosting came next, and she closed her eyes, wanting to savor the bite for as long as she could, as she was sure she had never tasted anything more amazing in her life.

"Well?" Steve mumbled through a full mouth, icing all over his face and his eyes twinkling with amusement as he set the rest of his cinnamon bun down on his plate.

Her eyes flew open, heat rising up her chest to settle in her cheeks, and set the confection down on her plate as she continued to chew. Once she swallowed, she answered, "I don't think I've tasted anything more incredible."

"Right!" Steve exclaimed, reaching over for some napkins and handing a few to her.

Both were a mess, and Emersyn couldn't help but laugh as she wiped at her face, doing a very poor job of cleaning up the sticky mess. Once she was sure she had gotten it all, she set down the napkin and reached for her tea.

"You've got a little icing in your hair," he said, his long, lean body reaching over the table and sliding his finger-tips down a ringlet resting against her face. Her body heated as he tucked the curl, now free of the icing, behind her ear, the pads of his index finger and thumb rounding her ear in a gentle caress. "That's better," he said, meeting her gaze. The gesture made unexpected tingles spread across her body. It was something so small, but at that moment, she was sure he saw her. The real her and the realization of that was terrifying.

CHAPTER 5

They had agreed to meet up on Saturday afternoon, Steve meeting her at her apartment. He parked on the street, her apartment part of a 6-floor complex on a busy street in Winnipeg. The brick building was old, but well kept, and as he walked into the lobby, he felt like he had walked into a swanky lobby caught somewhere in the early 1990s. All black lacquer furniture, mirrored glass walls and fake plants in the corner. He buzzed her apartment number, and she answered, the telecom crackling. "Be right down," she said, and he took a seat on the surprisingly comfortable lobby loveseat and waited patiently for her. Fifteen minutes passed, and he glanced at his watch, ready to buzz her again when the sound of the elevator chimed, and Emersyn walked out. She was wearing a short, tight, black and white plaid skirt that hit mid-thigh, a fitted white long-sleeve top that stretched perfectly over every curve, and was carrying a black jean jacket. She had her ringlets pulled up in a bun at the top of her head, with random curls cascading around her face, and on her feet were black Converse sneakers. Steve's mouth went dry as he took her in. She managed to look adorably cute and sexy all in one, and he liked what he saw.

He approached, unapologetically admiring the gorgeous woman in front of him, and she gave him a quick, reticent smile. "You look nice," he said, wanting to say so much more than that but immediately feeling a cool breeze wafting from her.

"Thanks," she said, feigning a smile but not making eye contact as she slipped on her jacket and started walking towards the door, not looking behind her to see if he was following.

Shaking his head, he sighed, and followed her, wondering why she had her guard up now.

* * *

EMERSYN WASN'T sure why she was acting like this. A total brat to the one guy that seemed to see and like who she was, just as she was. After their impromptu bakery date, she left feeling naked. Like he had stripped down her defences. It was a feeling she had never experienced before, and as he dropped her off at her car, she vowed she wouldn't let him do that to her again. It was too vulnerable a place to be and dangerous to let him get too close. The last thing she wanted him to see was her mess of a life.

Opening her door for her, she climbed in, still not making eye contact, knowing if she looked into those beautiful onyx eyes, she would lose herself again, and there wasn't much left of her to lose. Her entire world revolved around two things: singing and the care of her mother. There was no room for anything else. Let alone a man. At least, that was what she kept telling herself.

She directed him to the theatre, and after they parked, an acquaintance of hers from the costume department greeted them in the lobby. She led them through the theatre and backstage to a storeroom that was wall to wall racks of costumes.

"Our 1930s styles are this way."

They followed her to a back corner, and Emersyn rifled through the racks as she caught up with her friend, not once introducing Steve but handing him hangers and loading up his arms, like he was a human closet. Emersyn picked up a box of accessories, and they followed her friend out of the room, Steve following behind, balancing the big precarious pile of clothes in his arms.

"Put those on the rack over there." Emersyn ordered sternly, flitting her hand in the direction of the rack and still not looking him in the eye. "Then start bagging them up."

* * *

STEVE GLANCED OVER, seeing a stack of garment bags in the corner. He turned to her and blinked, frustration rising within his body. *Unbelievable. She's doing everything she can to dismiss me.* "I could use some help," he mentioned, abruptly interrupting the conversation she was having with her friend.

Emersyn whirled around, her hand on her hip, and

gave him an annoyed glare, the first eye contact she had given him all day as she said. "Can you give me a minute, Steve?"

Exasperated, with the heat of frustration surging through him, Steve awkwardly set the pile of clothes on the floor. Her friend stole empathetic glances over Emersyn's shoulder, watching him do his best as Emersyn continued their conversation completely ignoring Steve. One by one, he hung up the costumes on the rack, sorting them as he went, then covering them with garment bags. When Emersyn finally turned around, the task was done, and he was leaning against the wall, wiping the sweat from his brow. Her eyes met his briefly, and he could see a sliver of guilt in their depths. Just a glimmer that she felt bad for treating him the way she was and that she was doing this to erect a wall between them again.

Two can play this game. Steve pushed off the wall and grabbed each of the heavy garment bags, slinging them over his shoulder and walking towards the exit through the theatre. He didn't look back to see if Emersyn had followed, but he could feel her, her eyes boring into his back. When they exited the theatre, Steve went directly towards his SUV, and he opened the back hatch, dropping the garment bags inside and not looking her way as he unlocked the driver's side door and climbed into his vehicle. Depositing the box of accessories on the sidewalk, she tried to tuck the slew of garment bags in so she could close the hatch. He watched her struggle in the rearview mirror and could make out her face, one of a person that looked both sheepish and as frustrated as he was feeling. *Good.*

Hatch closed, Emersyn placed the accessories in the backseat, got into his vehicle, and he could feel her eyes on him as she put on her seatbelt. With eyes trained forward, his heart hammering in his chest, he battled to stand his ground and keep his frustration in check. Starting the vehicle, he pulled into traffic, trying to calm himself with a few deep cleansing breaths, not caring if she saw or heard them. *Do your worst, Em. I'm not backing down.*

EMERSYN COULD FEEL the sheer frustration and irritation radiating off Steve as they drove back to her apartment. Her plan to be abrupt and aloof worked a little too well, and now she sat here in the passenger seat, listening to him try to steady his breathing and temper the flare of fire that burned across his face. Pangs of guilt consumed her. He truly was the nicest guy and had driven all this way to help her with this task, and now she treated him like him going out of his way to help her meant nothing to her. She thought about her mom, and how she always treated people trying to help her or be kind to her. Her mother would always say, "Kindness is for the weak. We Bridgers are strong, take-charge women." She shook her head, thinking about her mother's words. *Can't you be strong and still be kind?*

Deep in thought, she hadn't noticed they had arrived and parked beside her apartment building.

"I'll help you carry the costumes inside. I can keep the box of accessories and bring those to Dee. The rest should fit in your car when you come to next week's practice." He said, his tone calm, yet still carrying an edge of annoyance to it.

She nodded, and they retrieved the garment bags. Reaching for one, he swooped in, taking it as their eyes met. "I'd appreciate it if you could get the door for me, please," he said cooly, his mouth in a firm line and his eyes indignant.

Leading him into her building, the tension palpable between them, they took the elevator to her floor as she guided him down the hall, stopping at her apartment door. She opened it, and he followed her into a small bachelor suite. Although her apartment was tiny, it was nicely laid out with a galley kitchen on the side, a little dinette separating the kitchen from the living room where a couch and chair sat across from a modest TV and stand. Next to the stand was a large bookshelf over-flowing with books, and a neatly dressed double bed was tucked into an alcove in the wall.

Steve tossed the garment bags over the back of the couch, and she internally cringed at his roughness, knowing how expensive these costumes were. Despite knowing full well that her behaviour had pushed him to it, she simply couldn't just stand there and bite her tongue any longer. "For fuck's sake, Steve! Those are valuable costumes. Are you determined to ruin them before we get them to Dee?"

Turning around quickly, he glared at her, his eyes dark, complete anger and frustration in their depths. "Now you care?" he asked, his voice low and growly as he crossed his arms over his chest. "At the theatre, you had no regard for those costumes, but now you care?" he asked, sucking in a deep breath between his teeth and letting it out like a hiss. The tension in his shoulders, obvious, he guffawed as he asked. "Why do you act like that?"

"Like what?" she asked, hand on her hip, pretending not to know what he was talking about.

"Like you loathe my presence?" he answered. "Like I'm just a lacky or go-for-boy."

She could feel the heat in her rise like a volcano ready to erupt, even though that was exactly how she had treated him. Yet, her fight-or-flight instinct kicked in when she questioned. "Why? Am I too assertive for you, Steve? Not used to a strong, take-charge woman?"

His hand flew up into the air as he huffed out a big breath in exasperation. Turning away from her, attempting to keep his composure, he turned back to face her again, his eyes so dilated that they were almost completely black. "I'm all for a strong woman. In fact, I find it sexy as hell, but there is such a thing as being a good and kind human being, and you, Emersyn, need a few lessons."

His words hit her in the gut. A low blow, a sucker punch, and yet as she stared into his indignant gaze, she deserved them. Emersyn had the ability to be kind, but she wasn't being kind to him, so she asked, "You don't think I'm a nice person?"

His eyes softened slightly as he replied, his voice steady. "I think you want to be, but you put on a mask, only showing a tough side. You act like being kind is a weakness when, truthfully, it's a strength." Silence fell between them, both glaring at each other, locked in a standoff of wills as he added. "You don't have to be tough all the time, Em. Not around me."

Standing there before him, the reality of her abhorrent behavior slapped her across the face as guilt and shame bloomed in her chest. Rogue hot tears pricked her eyes as deep emotion rose in her chest, threatening to suck up all the oxygen in the room. She hated to cry. She hated feeling weak. Blinking rapidly to keep the tears at bay, she squinted at him, so frustrated at being called out as she replied, "Fuck you, Steve."

Unfazed, he stepped closer, his stance strong, not backing down, his tone lowered and calm. "You can let your guard down with me."

She glared up at him, using every last defense at her disposal, coming up with the only thing she could think of that could make him stop. "Steve, if you don't stop, I'm going to scream."

He stepped closer, their bodies only a foot away from each other as he calmly challenged in a low, deep voice, "Then scream."

Steve had seen past her façade, and this made her angry, so fucking angry, she couldn't blink past the tears. "Stop fucking psychoanalyzing me!" she yelled, as traitorous tears streamed down her face. "Stop making me out to be my mother!"

Within seconds, Steve bridged the gap between them, his large warm hands cupping her face firmly but gently. Surprised, she looked up at him, meeting his gaze, seeing so much kindness and compassion where just moments ago there was annoyance, anger and frustration. "Stop Em." he whispered, his deep rich voice calm and soothing. "Stop trying to fight with me, you aggravating and beautiful woman. You don't have to hide from me. I won't hurt you."

She opened her mouth to protest but was silenced when he leaned down and brushed his soft lips to hers. The kiss was gentle, so gentle it made her want to weep, yet her tears stopped as unexpected desire ignited deep in her belly. She went on her tiptoes wanting more, and looped her arms around his neck, their height difference making her stretch to reach him. His hands left her face, and effortlessly he lifted her, cupping her behind with his large palms as she wrapped her legs around his waist. Carrying her over to the bed, he lay her down, covering her with his long, lean body, the intense heat of him sending her into sensory overload. He kissed her deeply, passionately, his tongue teasing her lips to part and let him explore as he pinned her to the bed with his weight. Tongues tangling and tasting, Emersyn was sure she could combust from kissing him alone. His lips left hers as he blazed a hot trail of kisses down her jaw, finding the sensitive spot between her neck and earlobe, nipping the lobe lightly, making her breath catch. Lifting himself off her, straddling her legs, he shed his jacket, and she sat up, pulling at his shirt, and helping him lift it over his head. Shirtless, she needed to stop to look at him, simply revel in the perfection that was his body. The rich caramel hue of his skin, more beautiful than she could have imagined as she took in his long torso, lean and toned. He was magnificent.

* * *

STEVE WAS TRANSFIXED as Emersyn trailed her fingers over the ridges of his shoulders, chest, arms, and torso. Letting her explore, her touch unabashed, as she traced every edge and angle. Leaning in to kiss her, his hands found the hem of her shirt, slowly lifted it over her head, and his pulse quickened as her white satin bra was revealed, that barely contained her ample curves. Dark, lustful eyes locked on his, she reached behind her back, freed the clasp, and slid the bra off, exposing herself to him. His eyes feasted on her breasts, large, taut and peaked, and his mouth watered as he took her in. *She's so damn gorgeous.* Eyes locked on his, Emersyn lay back, and he leaned over her, swirling his tongue around a dark tip as he tenderly caressed the supple flesh. She writhed under his ministrations, and a moan escaped her throat as he sucked and nipped lightly at the sensitive flesh. Lifting his head, their eyes met as he curled his fingers in the waistband of her skirt and slid it down over her sumptuous curves. "You are so damn beautiful." He said, wanting to admire her for a moment, her ebony skin glowing in the early evening haze as slivers of light danced across her perfect skin. Meeting her wanton stare, not seeing any sign of protest, he hooked his thumbs in the side of her panties, and slowly slid them down her legs. Bare and unveiled, raw need in her eyes, she reached up and pulled the tie holding her hair up, her ringlets spreading out above her head on the mattress like a halo.

This is her. The Emersyn she hid from the world, that she was sharing with only him. Meeting her eyes, a sense of reverence fluttered in his chest, honored that she would give him this gift and be so vulnerable. Tonight needed to be about her. What she wanted and needed. His gift in return.

Eyes not leaving hers, he reached into his pocket, removed his wallet, and took out a condom, tossing it onto the bed. Rising to her elbows, she watched as he rose from the bed, unbuttoned his jeans and slowly undressed. Sliding down his boxers, he stood before her naked. Her eyes slowly and unapologetically roamed south, lingering on his hard, steel length. She brought her bottom lip between her teeth as her eyes darted up to meet his dark desire in their depths.

Pulling at the tie holding his hair back, he let the long straight strands of his silky black hair fall past his shoulders as he demanded, his voice low and gravelly with need. "I want the real Em tonight. No masks. I want you to surrender to me completely. Can you do that?"

She stared wantonly at him, and he could see the war raging in her head. Despite this, he wasn't going to waver. He needed her to understand that he wasn't the enemy. Not her past childhood nemesis. Here in her apartment, he was just Steve, a man who deeply desired her and wanted her just as she was.

"This is only going to work between us if you trust me," he added, his intense gaze pinned on hers.

She closed her eyes and sucked in a deep breath, letting it out slowly. Her eyes blinked open, and he could see she had given up her fight. "I trust you," she breathed out, her voice husky with need.

Smiling at her words and knowing how hard it was for

her to concede, he climbed onto the bed, her knees falling to the side as he approached, making room for his body. She was slick and wet, and seeing the evidence of her desire for him made his pulse spike. His manhood twitched impatiently, wanting to sink deep into the warm softness of her body, but before he did, he needed to taste every inch of her gorgeous skin. Hovering over her, he kissed her hungrily, his lips melting with hers as he took her bottom lip between his teeth and nipped it lightly. A moan escaped her throat as he began to roam, his tongue tracking along her collarbone, and dipping into the hollow of her throat. He continued down between her breasts, his eyes meeting hers, dark as night and hazy with lust. "You have the most gorgeous breasts," he breathed out as he took a pebbled peak in his mouth, circled the tip with his tongue and sucked it in deep. She moaned loudly, her back arching off the bed with pleasure. He lavished the same attention on the other side and moved down her body, leaving a trail of kisses and love bites down her stomach, across hip to hip until he reached her apex, inhaling deeply the sweet musky scent of her arousal. Smoothing his hands up her inner thighs, he spread her wide, the glistening folds of her beckoning him as he took one long luxurious lap through her softness. *Sweet like candy.*

"Steve, oh God," she panted, gripping the comforter with her fists as she writhed under his touch. Her eyes cloudy with desire and her control sufficiently relinquished, it was his turn to make her lose all her inhibitions and just feel. Devouring her sweetness like a starving man, his tongue teased the sweet spot he knew would throw her over the edge as she unapologetically rocked against his mouth. With each indulgent swipe, she moaned, her sounds making him achingly hard and twitch in anticipation of the main event. As much as he wanted to be inside her, he wanted to give her this more. She needed to let go, release all the tension she held on to and simply give in to the pleasure he was offering her. Gripping his hair and tugging almost painfully, she chased her climax, teetering on the edge. Sensing her body needing more to tip her over, he slid two long fingers into her pulsing heat and crooked them, massaging her inner walls, as he took her sensitive bundle between his lips and sucked. Emersyn detonated, crying out in pleasure as she flooded his mouth with her arousal, her inner muscles rippling tightly over his fingers. Shuddering and eyes drawn tight, her back bowed as each wave of desire ebbed and flowed through her body. *God, that was beautiful.* Seeing this woman, who needed to always have control, turn into a puddle of satiation, he rose from the bed, reached for the condom and took it between his teeth, ripping the package open. This caused her eyes to fly open as she watched him sheath himself.

"I want you to feel good, Em. Tonight is about you," he said as he nestled himself into the groove of her body. "Communicate with me and tell me how you like it. Hard and fast or soft and slow?"

"Either. I just need you." She managed huskily as she reached for him, her hand curling around his over-sensitized member and making heat instantly ignite along his spine. Positioning himself at her entrance, he breached her, her eyes locked on his, as her body opened, accepting him, inch by glorious inch. She was so deliciously warm and tight, he wanted to roll his eyes back in his head, but he held her gaze until he was fully seated. They breathed together a moment, relishing the feel of their connection until he drew back, and she rocked her hips up greedily, begging for his return. Meeting her motion, their bodies colliding, his hair brushing the sides of her face, he swiveled his hips, slowly and deliberately as he drew out her pleasure and his own. The tightness of her body, the sweet friction of their connection — so intense he willed himself to keep focused, stay present, giving her what she needed. Her eyes locked on his with raw vulnerability in their depths as tears rimmed her eyes. Seeing she was fighting to keep them back; he leaned in and kissed her tenderly, his heart feeling like it might fracture for this beautiful woman beneath him.

"I'm sorry." She breathed out against his lips, her voice breaking with her words.

"I know," he replied, mirroring her emotion as the realization that she desperately needed this closeness and intimacy consumed him. He could see the loneliness in her gaze, the insecurity that she wasn't enough, and the deep - seated fear that she never would be. She was hurting, and she needed him. She needed his strength. Mouth hovering no more than a whisper from hers, he vowed, "I'll protect you, Em." She blinked, her long lashes fluttering with his words, as tears slid down her cheeks. Something poignant passed between them as they breathed each other's air, and he lowered his lips to kiss her again, this kiss sealing his promise to her. Trembling beneath him, both with emotion and unbridled desire, she closed her eyes, a moan escaping her throat as he quickened his pace. With the heat of his release threatening to ignite, he could feel she was on the cusp with him, and she needed permission to simply let go. "Em, come for me." he commanded with a growl as his orgasm ripped through him. With his order, she gasped, her pleasure capturing her, taking no prisoners as her body unravelled beautifully beneath him and her white flag raised in surrender.

CHAPTER 6

They lay there twisted up in her sheets, her head on Steve's chest, as his fingertips lightly brushed across her neck and collarbone. She had lost all sense of time and place, revelling in the feel of his long, strong body supporting hers. Something indescribable happened here tonight. Steve had managed to peel back her tough exterior and reveal the Emersyn she didn't let anyone see. The woman she wanted to be but wasn't sure she was. There were so few people she trusted, and she carried so much baggage from her childhood that it was easier to fall into what she was taught to be rather than what she wanted to be. She had to let go of the damage that she held deep within her. Damage that was so much a part of her psyche that it ate at her bit by bit, yanking her spirit and causing her to constantly relive the past. Somehow, despite her best efforts, Steve had figured her out. He had seen the woman behind the shield, and she was now at his mercy.

"I can feel you thinking," he said softly against her hair.

"I hope you aren't overthinking what's happening between us."

She looked up at him, her heart sighing as she met his contented gaze. "I'm not. I wanted this." she replied. "It's just, well...I guess I'm just scared I'll push you away."

He smiled, his lips curling up deliciously and making her want to kiss their sweet softness again. "I expected that, but you can do your worst, and I'll still want to be with you," he replied, pulling her closer and running his hand over the slope of her back. "I see you, Em. I see who you are in here," he said, resting his hand over her heart. "Let me show you what it's like to be cared for."

"How do you know I'm worth caring for?" she countered, raising her chin in challenge.

"Are you going to fight me at every turn?" he asked with a grin, then waggled his eyebrows. "Even after I gave you two orgasms."

"Maybe," she replied with a smile tugging at her lips.

He laughed, his deep chuckle making warmth flood her chest. She snuggled into him, feeling content and happy. *Yes, this is happiness.*

His stomach growled, reverberating against her skin, and she raised her head with a laugh. "Are you hungry? Seriously, what time is it anyway?"

Looking towards the window, the glow of the streetlights cast shadows on the apartment wall as she climbed out of bed, still naked, as she found her purse and fished out her cellphone. She turned to Steve, who was on his side watching her with appreciation, his head propped up looking all kinds of delicious tangled up in her bedding. "It's just after 8 p.m."

"We were busy." He smiled; his lips curled up wickedly. "What are you in the mood for?" he asked as he rolled himself out of bed and she watched him in all his naked perfection reach for his briefs and slip them on. He picked up his t-shirt and strode over to her. "If you could have anything you want, what would it be?"

She thought for a moment, his hands settling on her hips and bringing her closer as her mouth curved up in a naughty grin. "I want a big, greasy cheeseburger with everything on it."

"Now we're talking. I know just the place." He said with a wink as he handed her his shirt and turned to find his phone. Pulling it out of his jacket, he dialed and smiled at her as he ordered. "Hi, is it too late for delivery? No, perfect." he grinned as he ordered them two loaded burgers.

"And fries...can't forget the fries." She added as she slipped into his shirt. *If you're going to indulge, might as well go all the way.*

* * *

STEVE HUNG up his phone and turned to see Emersyn, now in his t-shirt, the hem hitting her upper thigh and stretching over her delectable curves. He reached for her hand and led her over to the couch, pulling her onto his lap so she could straddle him. His hands slid under the shirt as he gripped her behind, pulling her heat against his body. "I like seeing you like this."

"How's that?" she questioned, with a little laugh.

"All mussed up and well fucked." He replied with a naughty grin.

"You have a dirty mouth." She replied, taking her bottom lip between her teeth.

"It's not as dirty as my mind," he replied, his eyes darkening with desire.

Her lips curled into a smile as she rocked against his hardening body. Everything about being with her like this, making him ridiculously aroused. No woman had ever made him ache like this before. Their lips crashed together, a new wave of desire washing over them as his hands threaded through her thick curls and they kissed like they were parched and only they could quench each other's thirst. Breathless, she threw her head back, the sounds she was making raw and unrestrained as she ground her body against his.

"What are you doing to me?." she questioned, panting in his arms.

His lips curled into a smile as he kissed the side of her neck and made his way to the hollow of her throat. "You are so sexy," he growled out against her skin, making her shiver as she rolled her hips against the thick ridge constrained by his boxers.

"I have never had anyone turn me on this much." She breathed out, her chest heaving.

"Likewise," he growled out as he teased her earlobe with his teeth.

The loud buzzer of her apartment sounded, startling them both from what was sure to be round two. They both groaned, and she buried her head in his neck, sighing against his skin. Climbing off him, she sprinted over to the intercom to let the delivery driver in. Steve rose and reached for his jeans, putting them on and finding his wallet on the floor.

"I can get dinner," she said, reaching for her purse.

"No, I got it," he insisted, opening her front door, the delivery guy just getting off the elevator. He paid for dinner, carrying the takeout bag over to the dinette table.

"I'm not sure if you're being gentlemanly or archaic?" she said, squinting at him, a hint of a smile tugging at her lips.

"A little of both, I suppose, but you'll just have to get used to it." he threw back, cocking an obstinate eyebrow at her.

A smile slowly rose on her lips, and he could see she liked it when he challenged her too.

STARING down at the massive burger in front of her, Emersyn immediately regretted her choice. "This burger is so big, I'm not sure how to eat it." She said with wide eyes.

"The same way you ate the cinnamon bun the other day," he replied. "Pick it up and take a big bite."

She looked down at the gigantic burger, leaned back in her seat and furrowed her brows.

"What's wrong?" he asked, smoothing his hand over her shoulder. "Aren't you hungry?"

She cleared her throat, her eyes meeting his. "When I was growing up, I was never allowed to eat junk food or fast food. My mom would always say that kind of food was for the uncivilized, and if I ate it, I would get fat, and..." she quoted with her fingers, "...no one wants to see a fat girl on stage."

Steve shook his head incredulously, his mouth going into a firm line. "Come here," he said, taking her hands and lifting her to his lap as he curled his arms around her waist. "Listen to me when I tell you that indulging in something you enjoy is okay. Beautiful bodies come in every shape and size, and to me, you're perfect just as you are," he said, tucking a curl behind her ear affectionately. "You are so gorgeous; I can't believe I'm so lucky to be here with you. Trust me when I say this, that the big, mouth-watering burger over there is not going to change that." He smiled, his eyes flashing with mischief. "Besides, what's life without a little rule breaking?"

She liked his sweet words, and he was right. Having been weighed down by strict rules most of her life, her upbringing made something as simple as a little indulgence, that most people took for granted, so incredibly difficult for her. She was done following the rules; she needed to change the narrative.

Steve picked up his burger with one hand, its contents oozing out the side. He held it between them as chili dripped on his chest, and he held it close to her mouth, urging. "Take a bite."

"Are you feeding me?" she asked with a laugh, meeting his playful gaze.

"If I have to," he answered with mirth. "Make it a good one too, because if you're going to get dirty, then might as well get really dirty," he said, waggling his brows at her.

Opening her mouth, she took a big bite, the mix of

flavors bursting on her tongue, as a satisfied groan rose from deep in her chest.

"So good!" she exclaimed, her mouth full, and face smeared with chili and mustard.

"That's my girl," he said, pure amusement on his face, as he bit into the burger too, pulling a pickle out with his bite, letting it slap him on the chin.

Emersyn giggled as she reached for a fry and teased it towards his mouth, then popped it into her own.

"You tease," he replied as he brought her lips to his for a sexy and messy kiss.

They shared the burgers between them, feeding each other fries between bites and making a complete mess of themselves in the process.

"Pardon me, ma'am, I do believe you have a little something on your face," he said, swiping his tongue over the corner of her mouth to capture some of the ketchup.

"And you, sir, have something right there; let me get that for you." she said playfully, licking the chili that dripped on his chest.

Burying his face in her shoulder, he growled as he nipped her neck playfully.

"Steve," she squealed in delight as he licked his lips and gave her a coquettish grin.

"Hmm... delicious."

She met his gaze, her sides hurting from laughter and feeling more light and buoyant that she had in her life. "Thank you." She said, cupping his face between her hands and searching his eyes. "This has been the best time I've ever had."

He smiled, leaned in, and kissed her tenderly as he rose from the chair and cradled her in his arms.

"Where are we going?" She asked with a giggle.

"I think you and I both can agree that we feel a little dirty after that burger," he said, with a sexy wink. "How about a shower?"

"Will I get clean or dirtier?" she volleyed.

He stopped, locking his gaze on hers. "I think we can manage both, don't you?"

Her laughter was her answer as he carried her to the bathroom for the dirtiest shower she had ever experienced.

* * *

STEVE WALKED into the studio at Rami's house to find Rami and Savanah in a full-blown make-out session. Rami's shirt was off, but luckily Savanah was still fully clothed.

"Whoa!" Steve exclaimed, turning around quickly, and putting his hands up. "Sorry to interrupt."

"That's okay, Steve," Savanah reassured as she rose from Rami's lap and Steve slowly turned back around. "I was just about to leave so you guys can work." She said as she gave Rami a sexy "see you later" look and sashayed out of the studio.

Steve shook his head and started to laugh as he glanced over at his friend. "Sorry, I thought I would get here early. Didn't mean to cockblock you."

Rami rose from the couch, slipping his t-shirt back on, his smile wide. "Savannah wants to have a baby and has been insatiable lately. She literally came in here and jumped me," he said, pretending to dab his brow. "Not that I'm complaining, though.

Steve laughed and set his sheet music on the stand, looking up to see his friend, surveying him intently as he said, "Speaking of getting some. Have you been seeing anyone these days?"

Steve couldn't disguise his grin. He wasn't one to talk about his love life, and honestly, things with Emersyn were...he didn't even know what they were. With his timid smile, his tell, Rami clapped him on the back. "You don't have to tell me, but I can see something's changed. Not sure what it is or who it is exactly, but you look happier."

Am I happier? Generally speaking, Steve thought of himself as a happy guy, but this weekend with Emersyn, breathed new life into him. It had been so long since he had been with someone he really cared about, and being around her made him feel alive. Everything about her woke up his senses, and he couldn't get enough. Their combustible physical chemistry was addictive, and although it had been less than 24 hours since they had seen each other, he craved her already. Friday was the next practice, and he needed to find a way to spend more time together as there was so much more he needed to figure out about her. Firstly, he wanted to understand her relationship with her mother. The random things she said about her, controlling what she ate, what she did, keeping her from being a carefree kid. *What had her mother all done to her? Was she still part of her life? Was she still controlling her?* He had so many questions he needed answered, and without those answers, he was sure he would never fully capture her heart.

EMERSYN WALKED into Grandville Retirement Home, a spring in her step. The weight of the world, a little lighter on her shoulders after her time with Steve this past weekend. Last night, when Steve left, and she watched him lean against the wall waiting for the elevator after he kissed her senseless, she couldn't help but wish he could stay. Their brief time spent together was far more than she ever expected or thought she deserved. Steve made her feel desired and revered, like she was the most precious and beautiful woman in the world, and she wanted more time with him to explore their connection.

"Hey, Emersyn!" the front desk nurse greeted her, breaking her from her reverie. "Your mom is in good spirits today."

She breathed a sigh of relief internally as she didn't want anything to ruin this incredible high she was on.

Signing in, she made her way down the hall to her mother's room and knocked.

"Come in!" her mother sang out.

Constance Bridger was dressed in a sand-colored cashmere sweater and black slacks, a pair of beige low-heeled pumps on her feet as she hovered over a table she had in her suite. She had photo albums stacked on a chair and pictures strewn over the entire surface of the table.

"Hey Mom, what are you doing?" Emersyn asked curiously, loving the bright smile on her mother's face.

"I found my box of photos and I'm sorting them out." She replied happily. "Look at this one of you by the Christmas tree. Wasn't that the most beautiful dress?" She asked, holding it up for her to see.

Emersyn approached and looked at the picture of her in an emerald-colored dress, with so much tulle in the skirt she had a hard time sitting down. She remembered hating that dress but loving how much her mother fawned over her wearing it.

Her mother pulled back the picture and looked at it fondly, with so much joy on her face. "You were the prettiest little girl," she said as she brought the picture to her chest and held it to her heart, then looked at Emersyn, meeting her gaze. "And you still are so very beautiful." She said, reaching over to Emersyn and touching her cheek affectionately. "Can you help me sort these pictures out and get them into these albums?"

"Sure, Mom," she replied, pulling up two chairs for them to sit.

They sat together for the afternoon, her mother seeming to stay with her despite going down memory lane with each photo. It was times like this that gave her hope, that allowed the good memories to break through the clouds. Moments like this stowed the bad memories and made her feel a semblance of closeness to her mother. It was the best afternoon she had spent with her mother for as long as she could remember.

CHAPTER 7

$\mathcal{P}$ulling in next to Emersyn's car in the Primrose High School parking lot, Steve let the excitement of seeing her again envelope him. All week he found his mind drifting to memories of their night together, and although they had texted throughout the week, he felt the overwhelming need to hold her in his arms again. He needed to know if last weekend was a one-off or the start of something real. *Are we lovers? Are we dating? What does she want us to be?* In his mind, they were together, and he was hers if she would have him, but with Emersyn, she was still a bit of a conundrum, so he needed to prepare himself for anything.

Entering the gymnasium, he saw Oliver, Dee, and Emersyn deep in conversation, their brows furrowed, the conversation obviously a serious one. Emersyn glanced up at him, and her eyes softened as he approached.

"What's going on?" he asked. "You all look so serious."

"Anders." Dee replied, rolling her eyes. "He's been harassing Oli and Em again."

"What did he say?" Steve asked, his voice going deep and growly as he looked from Oliver to Emersyn, his intense gaze lingering on her face.

"He said he was happy we didn't bat for the same team so he could score with Emersyn. He also went into some..." he cleared his throat. "...creative explanative about certain body parts she possesses."

Instantly, steam rose to Steve's head, his face burning with anger as the uncontrollable need to punch Anders in the face took over. "Where's the asshole?" he asked, looking around and settling on the closed door of his office, hands in tight fists. "No one talks about my girl like that," he said, charging towards the office door.

"Steve, no, don't. Steve, baby, they were just words." Emersyn begged, getting between him and the office. "He's not worth it."

Steve looked down at her, his eyes going from shooting flames to simmering embers. She wrapped her arms around him and looked up, meeting his gaze. "I appreciate you wanting to defend my honour, but he's not worth it."

"I just can't stand that guy," he said, cupping her face affectionately.

"I know, baby," she said, going on her tiptoes and stretching to loop her arms around his neck, giving him a dreamy look in an attempt to defuse him "You're sexy when you're mad though."

Steve let out an exhaling laugh and leaned down, brushing his lips to hers for a chaste kiss.

Curling her arm around his waist, he pulled her into

him as they turned to be greeted by the very confused, and somewhat amused smiles of Dee and Oliver.

"Okay, let me catch up here." Oliver said, pointing back and forth between Steve and Emersyn. "You and the hunky rockstar here are a thing now."

Steve looked to Emersyn; his brow cocked in question, allowing her to take the lead. "Yes, Steve and I are dating." She replied with a smile.

Dee squealed, clapping her hands, and jumping up and down as she exclaimed, "I knew it!"

"Knew what?" Emersyn asked with a giggle.

"That you two would be great together." Oliver answered, Dee nodding in agreement.

Steve looked to Emersyn. As she met his gaze, her eyes asked for confirmation that he was on the same page as her. He reached for her hand, intertwining his fingers with hers and bringing her hand to his lips. She exhaled with a sigh, a relieved smile curling up her lips, and that was all that he needed to know she was his in return.

EMERSYN SLID onto the piano bench next to Steve, their practice done for the day. "Play me something," she requested, leaning her head on his shoulder.

Steve gave her a sexy grin, and asked, "Got any requests?"

She considered his question for a moment and smiled. "Play me something original."

"Well, there is a little thing I've been working on that I think you may like," he replied as he set his fingers on the keys. He closed his eyes and started to play, his fingers gliding, smooth and sure, over the keys. She closed her eyes too, feeling each note, rise and fall, an adage for sounds that strung together and touched her heart. She started to hum, feeling the tune come together in her mind as he played. It was beautiful, like two souls joining together in perfect harmony, and a swell of emotion rose high, making her want to cry. Emersyn closed her eyes because in that moment, despite all sense and reason, she was certain she was falling for Steve.

* * *

"I WANT to spend time with you this weekend." Steve declared as they exited the school hand in hand. "But I'll be in the studio recording all day tomorrow. We have a deadline to get this album done and are a little behind right now."

"I could come to St. Augustine," she suggested as she scrunched up her nose, looking unsure of his reaction. "I might have packed a little bag and brought it with me."

Steve laughed, all that doubt from earlier in the day about them, a distant concern. There was just one more thing he needed to put out there.

"So, are you telling me my girlfriend is staying with me tonight?" he asked, grabbing her waist and pulling her against him.

Her lips curled into a sexy smirk as she replied, "And tomorrow night, if you're lucky."

That's good enough for me.

* * *

STEVE PULLED up to a grey and white three-story character home on a quiet street just off the Main Street of St. Augustine. The street was lined with large oaks whose branches shaded each home protectively and made it feel like you were anywhere but a city.

"This is where you live?" she asked, her eyes trained on the big grand house before them.

"Not what you were expecting?" he asked, looking up at the home that stood like a historic beacon on his street.

"Not at all." She said, unfastening her seat belt. "It's gorgeous, Steve."

"It's been in the Furgallo family since my Grandparents bought it in the 1960s," he explained. "The building is broken into two self-contained living spaces. The top and bottom. My grandparents, or as I call them, Nonno and Nonni, live on the bottom, and I occupy the top and the loft."

He lives with family. I wasn't expecting that. Emersyn looked up at the large character home completely mesmerized by its classic beauty.

"My younger sister Raya and I were adopted into a large Italian family when we were two and four years old. My parents live down the street, and my sister lives with them. I have what seems like a million aunts, uncles, and cousins, and on holidays this house is filled with family and lots and lots of delicious food. I've lived here for five years and help my grandparents with yard work, general house upkeep and whatever else they need when I'm around. Others in the family take over when I go on tour."

There's a lot of information to unpack there. A million questions rushed through her head, but for now, she nodded and needed to know the answer to one question before she followed him inside. "Have you ever brought a girl home before?"

"You will be the first," he replied, meeting her gaze and seeing the apprehension in her eyes as he reached for her hand to reassure her. "My grandparents are a little crazy, a lot of fun and never meddle in my life. They're curious sometimes, but give me my privacy. They'll be thrilled that you're staying with me this weekend and will be excited to meet you."

Emersyn nodded. *You always wondered what it was like to be part of a large family, and ready or not, it's time to get a taste.*

They both got out of his SUV, and Steve retrieved her bag. Taking her hand, they walked up the stone steps to the covered front porch. Brass sconce lights flagged the large wooden front door and flicked on as they approached. He opened the door and gestured for her to enter as the most delicious smell of tomatoes, garlic and savory spices tickled her nose. She breathed deeply and looked up at Steve as she said, "Oh, my God, what is that glorious smell?"

Before Steve could answer, a sweet voice called out in question, "Stevie, is that you?"

"Yes, Nonni!" he called back.

"Oh, my sweet boy, come here and say hello to me and Nonno. I have a lasagna for you to take upstairs with you."

"Come meet them. I promise you they will be thrilled

to meet you," he said with a smile so big, Emersyn couldn't possibly say no.

He led her past the staircase and down the hall, towards the kitchen. A little woman, the same height as her, with gravity-defying perfectly coiffed white hair and a bright yellow t-shirt that said, "Chick," stood by the island smiling brightly. Her lips were painted a perfect cherry red, her eyebrows were penciled into a high arch, and she had the most gorgeous cheekbones Emersyn had ever seen. Although her face was lined deeply with years of good living, she could see the breathtaking woman from years before, shining through.

"Oh, my goodness, you have a friend with you," she said sweetly as she came around the island. "Tom!" she yelled. "Stevie brought home a girl."

An older man behind her shouted back from the living room, "I'm coming, Lucy!" He pressed a button on his automated recliner, making his chair rise slowly to help him stand.

Emersyn watched with bated breath as the elderly man was finally standing and he slowly shuffled over to his wife's side.

"Stevie brought a girl for us to meet," she repeated as he approached, his smile wide and friendly. Nonni was much taller than his wife, with a slight hunch, his shoulders broad and legs long. His face was a map of well-earned lines, and he had a warm, perfect denture smile. He wore a t-shirt that said, "Chick magnet," and Emersyn had to stifle a giggle at how incredibly adorable they were.

"Nonni and Nonno, this is my girlfriend, Emersyn

Bridger." Steve introduced proudly, giving her hand a squeeze.

"Girlfriend! Tom, our Stevie has a girlfriend!" Nonni exclaimed as if he was across the room.

"Goodness gracious, Lucy, I heard the boy," he said with bushy furrowed brows. "I'm not deaf."

"Sorry, Tom, I thought you might have forgotten your hearing aids again." She answered, rolling her eyes. "Hello, Emersyn, I'm Luciana Furgallo and this is my husband Tommaso Furgallo," she said, putting out her wrinkled hand.

Emersyn took her hand, her skin feeling like thin paper, but her nails were pristinely manicured and painted the same cherry red as her lipstick.

"Nice to meet you, Mrs. Furgallo, Mr. Furgallo," she said, shaking their hands.

Nonno brought Emersyn's hand to his lips and kissed it sweetly.

"Oh, stop it, you old flirt." Nonni chided, rolling her eyes again as she gave her husband a playful swat on the chest. "87 and still thinks he's 17."

Nonno flashed her a sly wink, making Emersyn smile.

"Please call us Nonno and Nonni," she said, as she strode over to the island and reached for a pan of lasagna far too big for two people. "Now you two, go eat this lasagna and canoodle as you young folks do."

"Alright, Nonni, thank you." Steve said, taking the lasagna and leaning down to plant a kiss on his grandmother's cheek. Nonni reached up and pinched his cheek firmly, giving it an affectionate tug. "So handsome!"

"And you, Bella Emersyn, are welcome here anytime!"

she said, giving her a chaste hug and then waving her hands to shoo them away. "Now go, get going. Nonno and I have a date with the Netflix."

Climbing the stairs to his upstairs suite, they reached a short landing ending in a wooden door. Steve fished keys out of his pocket, unlocked the door and gestured for Emersyn to step inside. As she did, he flicked on a switch, and the wide-open space illuminated with light. Emersyn's eyes widened and jaw slackened as she took in the expansive space where he lived. His place was something special, and it wasn't lost on him how lucky he was to live here.

"Would you like the grand tour?" he asked, setting the lasagna down on the kitchen island, and taking her hand as she nodded eagerly.

Situated in the corner was a kitchen, with granite countertops, and a large island set with four bar stools. The oak cabinets had been painted a sage green, and the color contrasted beautifully with the original red and brown brick chimney stack that ran along one edge of the cabinetry. Along the wall was a large picture window and bench, which provided seating on one side of a large wooden table. Across the room, built-in bookshelves framed another picture window and housed another bench for reading or lounging, whatever one preferred. He had a large sectional couch that sat opposite a large flat-screen TV mounted on the wall. And across on the other side of the wall was an old upright piano. Three rooms branched off the main space. Two empty bedrooms and a bathroom with a cast iron claw-foot tub that made Emersyn literally vibrate with excitement when she saw it. *Noted.*

"My bedroom is up here," he said, guiding her up the stairs to the loft. The space was large, with angled walls, and had a low-profile queen-size bed that sat on a dark wood platform, flagged by two alcove windows with bedside tables and lamps underneath. On the opposite side was another built-in bench with an assortment of pillows inviting one to sit and look out the window facing the back garden. In the room he had a wardrobe and a long dresser matching the dark wood of the bed.

"Steve, I'm seriously speechless." She said as she peeked out the window by the bed to see a view of the street through the large oak trees. "I never imagined you lived in a place like this."

Steve smiled and strode over to her, pulling her into his arms and wrapping her tightly. "I'm glad you're here," he said, sliding his hand along the back of her neck to tangle in her hair. "I missed you this week."

"I missed you too," she replied, knowing she had relived their night together countless times in her head. "I missed this body." She said, looking up at him through her long lashes, as she reached for the hem of his shirt. Loosening it from his jeans, she ran her hands underneath and up his long, lean torso. Reaching for his collar, he pulled the shirt over his head with one swift move, and the heat of his tanned skin radiated between them. Eyes locked on his onyx gaze, she leaned in and kissed his chest, then ran the tip of her tongue down, tracing his abs and dipping into his belly button.

"Em." he growled as he tried to pull her up, but she shook her head, a naughty grin on her face.

"Last time you were all about me, let me do something just for you." She said huskily as she popped the button of his jeans and gave him a little shove onto the bed. "I've been thinking about doing this to you all week." She confessed as she removed his jeans and boxers, leaving him bare.

He was rock hard, and his length twitched and pulsed against his stomach. Kneeling beside the bed, with her hands gripping his shaft, making another growl reverberate from his chest. Coming up on his elbows, he watched as she ran her tongue over him, root to tip, her eyes dark with desire. She raised her head and smiled, a wicked smile as she took him into her warm, willing mouth and sucked him in deep.

His vision blurred as she toyed and teased his aching member, circling, and drawing him deeper into her ready mouth again and again until the familiar burn of pleasure blazed a path up his spine.

"Fuckkkk," he drew out with a feral groan. Unrelenting, she played his body with precision, finding a pace that left him teetering on the edge. His body tightened as his climax ripped through him, and he let out a chain of nonsensical words. Emersyn, unwavering, drank down every drop of his release until his body relaxed. Sitting up, he lifted her to her feet, and pulled her on top of him, taking her face in his hands. He kissed her deeply, passionately, their tongues gliding together in a sensual dance. Pulling his lips away, he met her lustful eyes and breathed out, "Strip for me."

So AROUSED, Emersyn's body vibrated with need for him. All week, every time she closed her eyes, she saw his dark, seductive stare as he buried himself deep within her body, and she had to touch herself to relieve the tension. Steve was like a craving to her; one taste and she wanted more. Slowly she undressed, letting each inch of skin tease and taunt him, watching his body react with fevered attention. Fully naked, she pushed him back on the bed and crawled up his body to straddle his hips. His hard ridge slid between her soft wet folds, making her core throb for him.

"Protection is in the top drawer," he said roughly, his breaths coming out laboured.

"I have an IUD," she said. "And I've never gone without protection."

"I haven't either. Are you sure?" he asked, cupping her face with his hands, his focus on her intense with desire.

"I've never been so sure. I want nothing between us," she said, her gaze unwavering. "I'm falling for you, Steve, and I want this first to be with you."

His eyes searched hers for any doubt, and not finding any, a smile curved his lips as he replied, "I'm falling for you too, Em."

Breathless, she leaned down and kissed him tenderly, feeling her heart burst inside her chest. "Make love to me," she whispered against his lips. His eyes softened as she positioned herself, lowering onto him, eliciting moans of pleasure from their lips. The feel of him inside her was so overwhelmingly good, it made her thighs shake uncontrollably.

"Are you okay?" he asked, taking her face in his hands again, meeting her lustful gaze.

"It's just so good," she said breathlessly.

He rose to a sitting position, his eyes locked on hers, his arms around her protectively. "We're so good together," he said, their breaths mingling, hot and heady, as a sheen of sweat started to form on their bodies. She rocked over him, her movements deliberate and slow, the sweet grind making her skin burn and sizzle with each rock of her hips. There was no way they could get closer, their bodies, their minds, their souls connected in the deepest of ways. She looked into his onyx stare, and she knew in that moment that she wasn't just falling for him, she was hopelessly and helplessly in love with Steve. He held her tight, the rhythm of their bodies bringing them higher as they lost themselves to another crashing wave of pleasure. Riding the wave, and completely lost to the moment, her eyes locked on his and she rasped out words she had never said to another living soul. "I love you."

CHAPTER 8

*H*er words hung between them as they lay together completely spent, a mass of sweat and satiation. They breathed in unison, a reverent silence, thinking, and instantly Emersyn regretted saying those three words out loud. *Why did you say that? You know it's too soon.*

"I can literally hear you thinking." he said, his voice husky and deep.

Feeling a tidal wave of emotion wash over her unexpectedly, tears pricked her eyes, threatening to escape. She went to speak, but a painful hiccup came out instead, giving her mounting emotions away.

"Em are you okay, baby, honey, what's wrong?" he asked, rolling her underneath him and caging her in with his arms.

She thought she might drown as a barrage of tears overflowed on her cheeks and into her hair with no way to stop them. She hiccupped again as her body trembled and shook with her sobs. Steve scrambled to get them under the covers to create a cocoon of warmth in an attempt to comfort her. Wrapping her up, he held her securely against him, stroking her hair, until her sobs started to subside, and only little staccato breaths remained.

He lifted her tear-streaked face to meet his eyes, which were glistening with tears too.

Before he could speak, she said. "I know I'm a hot mess of emotions. I've enough baggage from my childhood to fill a moving truck, and I've a controlling mother that ruined any chance of a musical career by burning every bridge we finally crossed. I know I'm a lot to take on, a project some may call me, and I don't expect you to feel the same way about me that I feel about you. And..."

Steve held his finger against her mouth, halting her words and racing thoughts. "Are you done?" he asked, gently meeting her gaze, his eyes soft and sweet. He caressed her cheek, wiping away the remnants of wetness lingering there, and leaned down, kissing her tenderly. He pulled his lips away and met her gaze with so much adoration and love her breath caught. "I'm in love with you too."

Emersyn exhaled the breath she had been holding, and she started to laugh. She wasn't sure why exactly. Maybe because she was riding this rollercoaster of emotion anyway and needed to counter the tears. But she laughed, a feeling of pure happiness enveloping her like a hug. He started to laugh too and said, "You go from professions of love to emotional breakdown to laughing hysterically. I may need a manual to figure you out."

"I told you, I'm a hot mess." She said between her fits of giggles.

He pulled her tight to him, enfolding her in his protective arms as he replied, "Good thing I don't mind getting messy."

* * *

STEVE DREW EMERSYN A BATH, adding some Epsom salts his mom gave him when he was achy and sore from performing. He gathered whatever candles he could find around his apartment, which was a grand total of two, and told her to soak while he warmed up dinner. As he waited, he sat down at his piano, blank sheet music in front of him and a pencil tucked behind his ear. He played a few notes, writing in the tune he played earlier that day with Emersyn. He closed his eyes and heard her voice humming as he played, the sweet melody forming in his head. He could hear the song, hear her singing it, lyrics on his lips. He got up and fished out a notebook he stored in the piano bench and started to write; the words coming out in a rush. He never would consider himself a lyricist, but with each line he wrote, the song took on a life of its own.

He set the lyrics to the side of the sheet music and started to play, singing quietly the bridge he had just written.

I love you, but I hate you.
My head waring with my heart
I don't want to need you.
But without you, I fall apart.

"You have a nice voice," Emersyn said from behind him. He turned around, her face fresh and glowing in the light of the piano lamp. She had pulled her ringlets into a messy bun at the top of her head and had changed into a cute pair of cotton pajama shorts and a tank top.

"You look relaxed," he said, beckoning her over to come sit with him.

"So relaxed I may just live in your tub, if you don't mind." She said, taking a seat next to him. "What are you working on?"

"Just trying to piece together this song. I have the sheet music written up, mostly anyway, but these words came to me, so I wrote them down."

She picked up the notebook and looked at him, her face serious as she asked, "Is this how you see me?"

"Honestly, yes," he replied. "I see you're someone who feels things deeply and doesn't always trust or own her feelings. You question everything."

Emersyn blinked at him, and he could see her instinct was to argue, but she just sighed as she knew he had her all figured out. She looked back down at the lyrics and spoke. "You know it's okay to question things, right? To hold high standards for yourself."

"I'm not saying you shouldn't, but you need to give yourself a little grace too. I only know a little about your childhood from the bits and pieces you've shared, but I think you've had a hard time trusting what others tell you and you've had a hard time trusting in yourself. You say you're broken, but I don't think you are. I think you're fractured but not completely broken. You just need someone to carry the weight a bit for you so you can heal."

Emersyn stared at him; her gaze steadfast. In that moment, he wished he could read her mind. *Did I go too far, or did I just remind her that I'm paying attention?*

Her eyes softened as she leaned in and kissed him, her lips so deliciously soft against his as her hands slid into his hair. Pulling back, she cupped his face, caressing his cheek with gratitude in her eyes as she replied, "Thank you for seeing me."

EMERSYN SAT on a kitchen stool watching Steve float around his kitchen as he plated their dinner. The smell of the homemade lasagna made her stomach growl, but it was the gorgeous shirtless man wearing low-slung cotton pajama bottoms that was making her salivate. He had his hair down, long just past his shoulders, and although she had never given much thought to the length of a man's hair, something about it looked wild and untamed, adding to his all-around sexiness.

"You look like you want to eat me rather than this lasagna," he said, setting two plates down in front of them and taking a seat beside her.

"I can neither confirm nor deny," she replied, letting her eyes roam freely over his bare chest. "Don't let this go to your head, but you might be the hottest guy I have ever slept with."

"Oh, okay, am I supposed to take that as a compliment?" he laughed.

"Yes, of course." She answered with a giggle.

He turned to face her, obviously fielding questions in his head as he said, "We're both in our late 20s and I would expect us both to have some mutual experience under our belts, and just know your answer doesn't affect our relationship in the least, okay?"

"I know, and if you are asking how many men I've slept with, the answer would be enough to know what I want and what I don't want."

"Have you had any serious relationships?" he asked curiously.

She shook her head and turned to face him, meeting his gaze. "When I turned 18, I started to rebel, and I'm not proud of everything I did during that time, but I don't have any regrets."

"I understand that. I never really had a rebellious phase, but I was never stifled either." He replied. "My parents were always very open with us."

"What was it like being brought into such a big family?" she asked curiously, as she took a bite of her lasagna and moaned her approval.

"It was cool. I mean, I was a kid, and they never made me, or my sister, feel like less than their own children. My parents did their best, always encouraging us to explore our Indigenous heritage, which I appreciated even though we were part of a very Italian family. We sort of got the best of both worlds in many ways. Do you have any idea about your background?"

"I know a little, just bits and pieces my mom told me over the years. I know my dad was from France, and my mother moved to Canada from the island of St. Martin when she was a young girl. She did say once that my father was quite a bit older than her, but I don't know if they were ever married or what the details of their relationship was. I do know that we never seemed to struggle financially, so when I was older, I wondered if he was quietly supporting us somehow. The details were sketchy. She told me my father left us when I was just a toddler, and from then on it was just me and her."

"Do you ever think of finding him?" he asked, meeting her gaze.

"No. I'm sure he's moved on with his life. He was never a part of my life, so I don't really need to be a part of his. That is if he's still alive." She answered resolutely.

Steve nodded, settling his hand on her knee and giving it a supportive squeeze. She smiled and turned to her food, neither saying anything more about the subject. As she picked up her fork, she thought about what it would be like to know more or have a connection to a culture or maybe even another person. Growing up with only the influence of her mother and considering how strained their relationship was prior to her illness, many times she found herself wishing she was part of something more. *What would it be like to be a part of a large family? What would it be like to be part of Steve's family?* That thought surprised her, but as she glanced over at Steve and he met her gaze, with love and warmth in his eyes, she couldn't help but hope that she would have a chance to find out.

STEVE AND EMERSYN strode into the studio hand in hand, and as per usual, Rami and Layne were there, but Rex was nowhere to be seen. Everyone looked up as they entered, including their producer, Sean, who was playing back a track they recorded during the last recording session.

Rami and Layne approached them, both with wide welcoming smiles.

"So, this is the source of Steve's recent happiness." Rami said, his gaze drifting over to Emersyn.

"Guys, this is my girlfriend, Emersyn Bridger," he said proudly, looking down at her with love and adoration in his eyes.

"Girlfriend? I knew something was up with you." Layne said, putting out his hand. "Hi Emersyn, I'm Layne Stark, bass guitarist for the band."

Rami followed suit. "Ramiro Perez, lead singer, but my friends call me Rami. Nice to meet you, Emersyn."

"Em, please call me Em. Thank you for letting me crash your session." She said, looking around at all the equipment, the sound booth and control board, with wide eyes. "This is like a dream to be in a studio like this."

"Em is a brilliant singer and vocal coach. She's also done lots of musical theatre." Steve bragged. His band-mates and producer nodded and were noticeably impressed.

"Wow, do you want to check out the sound booth before we start? I mean, we have time, and we're still waiting for our drummer to arrive." Rami offered.

Emersyn looked up at Steve and back to the producer, who gestured for her to go ahead. Steve followed her inside the booth and watched as she looked around, her eyes full of wonder. She touched the microphone and glanced at Steve, a huge smile on her face.

"This is all so amazing." She said, her voice breathless, her eyes glossy.

"Sing something," Steve encouraged, turning on his keyboard.

"Are you serious?" she asked.

"Yes! Hey Sean, Em is going to sing us something, okay." Their producer gave him a thumbs-up through the glass. Glancing back to Emersyn meeting her gaze, he added, "Sing whatever's in your heart."

She looked up at the mic and turned to Steve. "Do you know "Listen" by Beyonce?

"I do," he said as he started to play.

Closing her eyes, Emersyn stepped up to the mic, and Steve was transfixed as the first glorious note caressed from her lips. Glancing towards the guys watching on the other side of the glass, he smiled, their eyes trained on her as well. Overwhelming emotion rose in his chest as she sang; the ache in her voice, breaking his heart. She could have written the song herself, the lyrics ringing true for a life she had lived. A life where she wasn't heard and could only be what she was told to be. This was who she was, right here in this sound booth. A remarkably talented, beautiful force of nature who was slowly finding her own voice. As the song carried into the crescendo, a decision had been made. He wanted to collaborate with her, and he would do everything in his power to make her musical dreams come true.

* * *

THEY SNUGGLED ON HIS COUCH, an empty pizza box in front of them on the coffee table, his head in her lap as a random old movie played on the screen. Steve was exhausted. Studio days were always long and were made longer today with Rex's late arrival. Something serious was up with Rex, and when he came in over an hour late, he took one look at his friend's bloodshot eyes and knew he had been doing more than just drinking.

Emersyn had pulled his hair out of its tie and was running her fingers languidly through his long silky strands, making his scalp tingle with sensation. "Thank you for bringing me today. I really enjoyed seeing how it all worked and what your process was. It was exciting to be a part of it." she said happily. "Your bandmates are so nice too, even Rex, who hit on me by the way."

Steve laughed. "Take it as a compliment. He's hit on all our girls. I can't wait for you to meet their wives."

"Okay, let me see if I've got this straight. Savanah, who is Dee's best friend, is married to Rami and, apparently, she is on a baby-making mission."

Steve laughed. "So, he's telling everyone. Personally, I think he's enjoying the process a lot.

"I mean, who wouldn't?" she added, wiggling her eyebrows. "Then there's Layne who is married to his high school sweetheart, Juliana or Juli, who moved here from Hamburg, Germany, a few years ago. They have a little girl named Tabitha. So cute! He showed me pictures." She shared.

"He's a very proud papa." Steve laughed as he met her gaze.

"And then there is Rex, who is single and ready to

mingle, his words not mine, and he hooks up with a girl named Charlene, that I gather no one is fond of," she finished.

"Unfortunately, yes. Since our last tour, they've been seeing each other on and off, and if you ask me, she's bad news."

"Are you concerned about him?" She asked, giving him a wary look.

"I am. I didn't like the way he looked today. A little too glassy-eyed and lethargic for my liking. I think I need to talk to the guys and ask their opinions. We may need an intervention," he said, his voice full of concern. "We may be a rock band, but we as a rule keep our noses clean."

She nodded, sifting her fingers through his hair, and giving him a compassionate smile. "I can see how close you all are."

"They are family. Family doesn't always need to be blood, and they are my brothers."

Emersyn sighed contentedly, which quickly turned into a yawn. Steve rose from the couch and put his hand out to her. She accepted, and he pulled her to her feet, bringing her body flush with his. She smiled up at him through her long eyelashes. He slid his large hand around the back of her neck and leaned down to kiss her sweetly. Teasing her lips open with his tongue, he deepened their kiss, the raw passion between them igniting into a fire.

"Take me upstairs." She breathed out against his lips as he lifted her and carried her up to his bedroom.

CHAPTER 9

Dreams are a beautiful thing. Especially when you wake up with the girl you're head over heels in love with on top of you, naked and ready, planting sweet kisses all over your face to wake you up.

"Why hello there, sexy," she purred, raking her fingers over his chest. "You're finally up." She said, emphasizing the "up."

Steve chuckled groggily, his body obviously awake before he was and ready for a little morning delight. Taking in the beautiful woman straddling his hips, dirty thoughts ran through his head, and he gave her a wicked grin. "Turn around and straddle me again, then take me deep," he ordered. "I want to see that gorgeous ass."

Having noticed and appreciated all her curves, he had developed a particular fondness for the shape of her backside. She did as he asked and sank onto him, letting out a long-drawn-out moan as she did. He gripped her hips, his fingers digging into the supple flesh as he guided her rise and fall over the length of him. The erotic sight of them connected her sensuous sounds and the tight rippling heat of her inner muscles, pulling him deeper, causing his body to burn with desire. She bowed her back, and he cupped her breasts, teasing their peaks as she ground on him with a steady rhythm, taking them both higher. The slow burn of his climax on the horizon, her sensual tease and impatient to get her there with him, he flipped them over making her squeal and moan loudly as he gripped her hips firmly, thrusting into her from behind, the sound of their skin making contact echoing through the loft as he took her body hard and fast. Crying out, she gripped the pillow as she gave in to the pleasure and screamed out his name. With the sound of his name on her lips, her orgasm caused a chain reaction through his body like a surge of electricity, all circuits connecting as he let go. With heaving chests, he brought her flush with him, her back to his chest, needing her close, needing to hold her to his heart.

Clinging to her body, he kissed her shoulder and trailed love bites along the column of her neck.

"No one has ever played my body like this," she declared with a sigh as she melted into his chest and glanced up at him, her eyes clouded with satiation. Gripping her chin, he brought his lips to hers in a sensual kiss as she shivered in his hold.

"Cold?" he asked as they collapsed onto the bed and he reached for the comforter to cover their sweat-laden bodies. Pulling her tightly into him, their combined warmth was blissful and satisfying. He had never been with anyone that he felt this in tune with, mind, body and soul. Emersyn was like music to him, notes coming together to make a perfect melody. Their physical chemistry as natural to him as creating music. Smiling into her shoulder, he tenderly laid kisses over her heated skin as the notes to a song, their song, danced in his head.

* * *

THE LOUD BUZZING of a phone woke them from a deep sleep. Steve peeled himself from the soothing warmth of Emersyn's body and reached for his phone on the nightstand.

"Hello," he answered groggily, as Emersyn, turned and wrapped herself around him, sighing contentedly against his bare chest.

"Hi Stevie!" his mother chimed on the line. "Did I wake you?"

Lifting his head, he glanced over Emersyn's head to his alarm clock. 11:12 a.m.

"Yeah, but we should be getting up," he replied, running his hand through his hair.

"Is Emersyn there?" his mom asked.

That didn't take long. Shaking his head, he laughed, not surprised that the word had gotten out.

"Nonni called me yesterday." She said, reciprocating his laughter with her own. "Your dad and I were wondering if you two wanted to come over for lunch. I would love to see her again."

Emersyn raised her head, resting her chin on his chest,

obviously hearing his mother through the phone. He glanced at her, apprehension in her midnight eyes.

"Let me talk to her, and I'll text you back."

Hanging up his phone, he pulled Emersyn in and wrapped his arms around her, securely uncertain if she would flee when he made his request.

"That was my mom. You and I are officially the talk of the family," he informed with a deep chuckle. "She just invited us for lunch." Another wave of uncertainty washed over her face, and Steve could see her trepidation immediately. "Speak to me. What are you thinking?"

She sighed deeply and lay her head back down on his chest as he stroked her hair, waiting for her answer. Lifting her head to meet his expectant gaze, her midnight eyes were glossed over with sadness as she replied. "I'm scared they're going to judge me," she said simply. "I know full well how terrible my mom was to your family, especially your mom, and I'm worried that they'll take one look at me and say, the apple doesn't fall far from the tree."

"Are you scared they won't approve of us?" he questioned to clarify as he searched her face for the answer.

She nodded with unease. "I can't tell you how many people won't talk to me because of the things my mom has said and done. She burned so many bridges, and if I'm being honest, I'm completely embarrassed by it."

Squeezing her tightly to his body, he sucked in a breath, his mind reeling as he formulated his response to her concerns. If they loved each other, his family would at some point come into the picture. They were a huge part of his life, and he wanted to share them with her. He knew who they were, and she needed to trust him, that he wasn't about to feed her to wolves. "You need to know something about my parents. They are very forgiving and believe in grace. They also know that people are responsible for their own words and actions, and you were just a kid. You weren't responsible for the things your mother said and did."

Emersyn sighed dramatically as she wiggled out of his hold and swung her legs out of bed. "I wish it were as cut and dry as that, but it's not that simple," she answered, rising from the bed. "You can text her back that we can go for lunch. I'm going to take a shower."

STANDING UNDER THE SPRAY, Emersyn let the warm water of the shower run over her, as hot tears pricked her eyes, mingling with the droplets running down her body. She closed her eyes, trying to steady her breathing as her curls clung to her face in wet tendrils. Emersyn's mind was in a dark place, a place she hated to go. For the past 10 years, she had to fight to come through the dark cloud that was her mother. By her actions and words, she had isolated them and left her with a barrage of insecurities and anxieties resulting from her mother's constant negativity and control. Now, something as simple as meeting the parents of the man she loved was triggering her anxiety, and for that, she resented her. She resented her for all the ways she had damaged her in the past and now for being sick.

Resentment and guilt, mixed with anger that she could never break away fully, even if she wanted to. And all she was left with was this nasty mix of emotions to make sense of.

Thinking back to all those competitions, her mother turned up her nose to the other moms and said nasty things to them. Even as a child, she knew her mother was a bully, justifying her behavior as wanting the best for her daughter. Using her as an excuse for unnecessary meanness resulted in others painting her with the same brush.

The fact that today she would come face to face with her mother's main target was almost too overwhelming to think of. Remembering how incredibly gracious Mrs. Furgallo was and how she used to watch Steve and his mother, envious of the maternal love she bestowed on him and his complete adoration for her. Many times, she wished she had that kind of relationship with her own mother. Instead, she was given only tidbits of love, and it was always conditional.

The shower door opened, and Steve's strong arms came around her shoulders. She leaned back against his chest, letting the tenderness of his embrace and the love in her heart radiate through as she sighed. *You are such a mess, Emersyn. You need to tell him about your mom. He needs to understand what he's getting himself into here. He needs to understand that you will always be controlled by her. Even though now not by her words and actions but by her disease.*

IT WAS hard to fully understand Emersyn sometimes. Steve understood how she was a product of her childhood and more than understood how embarrassed she was by how her mother treated others, but what he didn't understand was why she still carried on a relationship with her. From her confessions, she carried so much animosity towards her mother, and yet her mother was still a part of her life. It didn't fully make sense to him, and he couldn't help but wonder if there was more to their story than what she was telling him.

They walked hand in hand down the street, towards his parent's place, Emersyn looking more and more anxious with each step closer to his childhood home.

He squeezed her hand for reassurance and gave her a comforting smile. "It's going to be okay; trust me on this."

Rounding the cul-de-sac, they stopped in front of the blue house, and she tensed next to him. Turning her to face him, he cupped her face in his hands. "Just show them who you are, Em. They will love you; I know they will." Leaning down, he kissed her chastely, and her body eased with the tender brush of his lips. Searching her eyes, he smoothed the tension crease between her eyebrows with his thumbs, producing a faint smile. "If you feel anxious or need reassurance, just touch me or take my hand," he said, reaching for her hand again and leading her up the walkway to the front door. The door flew open, his mother standing in the doorway.

"Emersyn!" she exclaimed as she skipped down the steps to meet them. "You're all grown up and so beautiful!"

Emersyn looked at Steve with a combination of

ambivalence and surprise as his mother pulled her in for a hug and he mouthed to her, "I told you."

"Mom, let her come into the house, for goodness' sake." Steve chuckled, reclaiming Emersyn's hand, and giving it a supportive squeeze.

"Yes, please come in! Welcome to our home!" his mother said, leading them into the house and into the main living space. "Raya is going to be home later, so it looks like it's just the four of us for lunch. I hope BBQ and salads are good enough. Dad's out back by the grill if you want to say hi."

Steve led Emersyn through the open-concept kitchen, past the living room and through to the back patio where his father stood at the grill, light blue button-down shirt sleeves rolled up and a big BBQ turner in his hand.

"Stevie!" he acknowledged as his eyes drifted over to Emersyn. "And this must be your girlfriend, Emersyn."

"Does everyone know we're dating now?" Steve asked with an incredulous laugh.

His dad reached into his pocket and held up his cell phone. "Family group text. No one should have taught Nonni how to text. She sent everyone two rows of heart emojis and the words, Stevie has a girlfriend. My phone has been buzzing all weekend." His dad chuckled as he turned to Emersyn and put out his hand to her. "We're very happy to have you here."

Steve glanced over at Emersyn, who accepted his father's warm greeting, but he could see the cautious tension in her stance and apprehension in her eyes. As much as he reassured Emersyn that his parents didn't hold her accountable for her mother's words or actions, he could feel the nervousness circulate around her like a looming thunderhead. A storm of anxiety ready to unleash. The worry gutted him as he studied her and asked himself, *Will she shut down and let her insecurities take over?*

THE FURGALLO HOME was filled with family photos on what seemed like every surface and wall. Photos of the four of them laughing, making funny faces, and grinning from ear to ear. Photos from vacations, family gatherings, birthdays, and holidays. She had never seen so many photos. Each one laid out as reminders of joyful memories they shared together as a loving and devoted family.

Feeling the anxiety rise in her body, Emersyn reached for Steve's hand, gripping it firmly. Putting his arm around her, he leaned into her ear, whispering, "Are you okay?"

She nodded, feigning a smile, but she was anything but okay. His parents were so nice, so welcoming and seemed thrilled that they were dating, but the more she looked around at all the photos of smiling faces staring back at her, mocking her, she wasn't sure she belonged here, and that realization sat like a stone in the pit of her stomach.

"Emersyn, are you still singing?" His mother asked curiously. "You always had the most beautiful voice."

"I...I... yes, I still sing." She answered, stuttering on her words. *Emersyn stop stuttering. You don't want to sound stupid and uneducated.* Her mother's words echoed in her ears, and she could feel her pulse pounding in her head.

"Excellent!" his mother exclaimed, taking a bite of her potato salad.

"You should hear her now, Mom. You thought she was amazing as a little girl; her voice will blow your mind. It's so incredible." Steve added proudly, his hand on her knee giving it a squeeze.

"I for one, would love to hear you sing again." His father added. "Perhaps after lunch Steve could take to the piano and you could sing us something."

This is too much, too much. They are very nice. Far nicer than I deserve. She tried to blink, her eyes burning, wanting to release tears, and her pulse spiked, sure her heart was going to jackhammer right out of her chest. *Nice is for the weak, Emersyn.* Haunts of her mother's words jumbling her thoughts. *Shut up, Mom, shut up!*

Bile rose in her throat, and Emersyn felt nauseous, her stomach ready to seize. Abruptly she rose to her feet, her chair making a loud scraping sound across the concrete patio. "Excuse me, where would I find the washroom?" She asked, trying to keep her voice steady, her body about to unleash a full-blown anxiety attack.

"When you go inside, turn right down the hall, and it's the first door on the right." His mother answered her, a mix of concern and confusion on her face.

Rushing through the patio door and down the hall, she found the bathroom right away and closed the door behind her. Dropping to her knees by the toilet, her stomach convulsed and roiled as her lunch came up into the bowl. Internally groaning, she flushed the toilet and sat back leaning against the opposite wall, closing her watering eyes, and trying to will the nausea away. *Why are you doing this to yourself? Why did you take your guard down? Steve doesn't deserve to be with someone like you. Someone who has so much baggage.* Stinging tears pricked her eyes as she tried to breathe deeply in and out to steady her racing heart.

Losing track of how long she sat against the wall, her arms wrapped around her legs as she tried to pull herself together, head bowed against her knees. It wasn't until she heard a gentle knock on the bathroom door that she broke from her trance. It opened slowly, and a beautiful woman with dark onyx eyes just like Steve's and long flowing black hair peeked in.

"Oh, sorry, I didn't realize someone was in here." She said, staring down at Emersyn, curled up on the bathroom floor. She hesitated a moment in the doorway, then slipped inside, locking the door behind her and slid down the wall to sit next to her. They sat there in silence for a few minutes, no words passing between them until the woman turned to meet her gaze and smiled. "You must be Emersyn. I remember you."

Emersyn groaned audibly, feeling her stomach tighten again, and she scrambled to her knees, leaning over the bowl again. Without hesitation, the woman grabbed her hair and held it back for her as she heaved the rest of her lunch into the toilet. Flushing, the woman rose to her feet, reached into a cabinet and pulled out a washcloth, wet it under the cold water of the faucet and handed it to Emersyn.

"Feel better?" She asked, giving her a concerned smile as she watched her get to her feet and dab at her face. "I know it's not the best time for introductions, but I'm Raya, Steve's sister."

"I'm sorry you had to see that." Emersyn apologized, feeling heat rise to cheeks, completely embarrassed.

"Don't sweat it." Raya said, waving her hand in the air and shaking her head. "Seriously, I understand you probably better than you think. You're feeling overwhelmed and a little anxious, I'm guessing."

Emersyn nodded and leaned over the vanity, glancing up to meet her wary reflection in the mirror. "I'm not sure what's wrong with me. I feel like a complete disaster."

Raya gave her an understanding smile and reached into a drawer, pulling out a new toothbrush and some toothpaste, handing it to Emersyn. Accepting it gratefully, she watched with interest as Emersyn brushed her teeth and dabbed her face again with the cool washcloth.

"You know, we've all got some baggage around here, right?" Raya said as Emersyn met her eyes in the mirror. "Steve and I didn't exactly have the best start in life, and I know Steve has dealt with residual memories from back then. If it weren't for the Furgallos we likely wouldn't be here today." Emersyn turned to face her leaning against the vanity as she continued. "I know my parents are so nauseatingly sweet, and even I have times where it's hard to keep my lunch down." She joked with an amused roll of her eyes as her gaze met Emersyn's and morphed to earnestness as she added. "But they're sincere too. It's not an act or something they turn on and off. They're just good people with no agenda."

Emersyn turned to face Raya, one question swirling through her head that she needed answered. "Do you think they look at me and see someone that needs to be fixed?"

Raya swiped her hand through the air to dismiss her question. "Not a chance. They accept you, scars and all." She added, reaching for Emersyn's hand and giving it a supportive squeeze as a smile curled her lips. "Besides, if you're going to be my sister one day, you've got to be a little flawed and crazy like the rest of us," she added with a wink.

Before Emersyn could process her comment, Raya opened the bathroom door and pulled her down the hall and back to the patio.

Steve's eyes rose immediately to meet them, and he gave Emersyn a concerned look before his eyes drifted to her hand being held by Raya's.

"Raya, come have a seat and join us." Mr. Furgallo encouraged. "I see you've met Steve's girlfriend, Emersyn."

"We did," she said, looking over at Steve and giving him a playful grin. "Although I can't even begin to see what she sees in a dork like you, Steveo."

"Dweeb," Steve replied, as Emersyn came back to sit down next to him and Raya took a seat beside their mother. Emersyn met Steve's questioning gaze, the building tension that was there before seeming to have eased as she turned and glanced around the table at his wonderful family. He threaded his fingers through hers, and a smile tugged at Emersyn's lips, knowing he understood and had her back.

* * *

STEVE WASN'T sure what his sister had said to Emersyn, but from the moment she walked back out onto that patio, he could see the air around her shift. Leaning over the kitchen island, he watched as Emersyn and Raya sat together on the couch laughing as she showed her photo albums of them as kids.

"I like her, Steve," his mother said quietly as she sidled up next to him. "You two fit well together. Like two puzzle pieces. It's nice to see."

Steve rose to his full height and let out a long exhale as his gaze met Emersyn's from across the room and she flashed him her beautiful smile. "I'm in love with her mom," he said simply. "I've never felt like this before."

"Does she feel the same way?" His mother asked, looking him in the eye, a grin brightening her lovely face.

"She said it first, so yeah, she does." He replied. "We've literally only dated for a week though. Are we insane to feel so strongly for each other this soon?"

"No, not at all. I knew I loved your dad quickly. I mean, I went from hating him to loving him within a span of a week." She replied with a nostalgic smile.

Steve turned to face her and laughed in disbelief. "Seriously? You and Dad always seem so in tune with each other. I don't think I've ever seen you two of you argue."

His dad took that moment to walk in from the patio carrying the last of the dishes from lunch, glancing between Steve and his mom curiously.

"I was just telling Steve how we couldn't stand each other when we first met."

His dad smiled, set down the dishes in the sink and reached for his mom, wrapping his arm around her waist and pulling her to his side. "I believe your exact words were, "I loathe you, Antonio.""

Steve's eyes grew wide, and he looked at his parents with amusement, wanting to know more.

"I met your dad at a college party and thought he was this totally arrogant jerk. Far too good-looking and so full of himself." His mom explained.

"And I saw her and thought she was the most beautiful girl I had ever seen, and why would she not want to go out with a handsome guy like me?" he said, with a cocky smile as he shrugged with a deep chuckle. "I agree; I was a bit of an ass back then."

"But then, he kept coming around and..." she started.

"... I wore her down," he finished as he wrapped his arms around his wife and planted a tender kiss on the temple. "I knew from the moment I laid eyes on Dahlia that she was the one for me."

Steve looked at his parents, the love they shared enviable, and he turned, his gaze drifting to Emersyn, wariness clouding his gaze as he shared. "I don't think she thinks she's worthy of me, though. She has so many insecurities, and her mom still has a very firm hold on her life."

"Does she talk about her?" his mom asked, compassion in her tone.

"She does, and it's very evident that she wants to break free but feels she can't." He said, furrowing his brows. "But I feel like there is something she's holding back from me regarding her mom. I just can't figure it out, though."

His mother rubbed his back and offered him an empathetic smile. "All you can do is be patient with her, Steve."

Steve knew his mother was right. He needed to be patient with Emersyn. She was still so closed off, and although she was starting to trust him, he could see there was still so much she was holding close to her chest. *How can I get her to trust me fully?* Glancing at Emersyn, realization dawned that he needed a plan to get her to talk so they had a fighting chance of making their relationship work.

CHAPTER 10

*W*alking out of Grandville Retirement Community, Emersyn smiled, thinking about her conversation with her mother. She was having a good day, and that meant a good visit. Her mother, seemingly more settled lately, hadn't asked about money in a few weeks now, and although she had slipped back in time during their visit, no negative memories had been relived, so for that she was grateful.

Emersyn didn't want anything to break her blissful bubble. The past weekend with Steve meant everything to her. Everything. Steve had invited her into every aspect of his life, introducing her to the people that mattered most to him, and they all welcomed her with open arms. *What if you and Steve work out and end up together? Then they would become your family too?* After dealing with the roller coaster of emotions she felt this weekend, the thought of that both scared and excited her. *Steve and I. Steve and Emersyn Furgallo. Emersyn Furgallo.* So many times, she wanted to change her last name, anything to not be a

Bridger. *Bridgers do this; Bridgers don't do that.* She had heard those phrases so many times in her life she wanted to scream. So many rules that never made sense to her. She shook her head, trying to shake off the memories. Maybe her and Steve could create their own memories together.

Her phone rang as she got to her car and unlocking it the call display read an unknown number. "Hello," she answered.

"Hey, Emersyn. This is Garrett Smithfield, Savanah Smithfield's brother and a co-worker of Dee's at Primrose High."

"Oh, hi, what can I do for you, Garrett?" she asked, surprised by this unexpected call.

"I know you're helping Dee with the Spring Musical, and we have a serious problem." he answered, his voice woeful. "We came into the school today to find all the sets destroyed. It was bad, Emersyn. Someone completely ripped them apart."

Emersyn brought her hand to her mouth in shock, her concern instantly going to her dear friend. "How's Dee? She must be devastated."

"She is, and I'm rallying friends and family to come out this afternoon after school to help start the rebuild. We need as many people as possible as we're hoping to get it all done tonight. I was wondering if I could count on you to come out. I know it's last minute, and I understand if you're unavailable."

"I'll be there, Garrett, anything for Dee," she answered without hesitation. Her phone buzzed with a text, and she glanced at it–Steve. *Word must have gotten out.* Garrett gave her the time they were all meeting, and they ended their call. She opened Steve's text, which read:

I don't know if you heard, but the sets are destroyed. I have my suspicions who it could be. Fucking Anders. See you at the school soon, babe. Love you.

Anders. He had been a thorn in their sides since the preparations for the musical started and had made it very clear that he was opposed to the entire thing. If Anders had something to do with this, surely there would be hell to pay.

* * *

STEVE PULLED up to Hastings Hardware, Rami waiting outside for him, with several other men he recognized from the community. He got out of his SUV, and everyone turned their attention to him. Rami made the introductions. Ben and Hayden Hastings, Davis Baxter, Jaxon, Cade and Owen Isley were all there to help with the rebuild, and more were gathering at the school. They all loaded their vehicles with tools, paint, lumber, and anything else they needed to recreate the sets.

Steve turned to Jaxon, his face serious and a little ashen. "Does Dee know who was responsible?" he asked.

"She's pretty sure it's Anders, but how do we prove it?" Jaxon asked with a resigned shrug. "The security camera had been tampered with, and I mean other than the guy being a grade A asshole, without it we don't have any concrete proof that it was him."

Steve shook his head. *There must be a way to prove this.*

The caravan of workers pulled up to the school,

occupying the now empty bus loop. Emersyn, Oliver, Layne, and Savanah were waiting at the school entrance as all the men approached, loaded up with tools and supplies.

"The principal already knows we're coming, and security has been informed." Savanah said, grabbing a can of paint from Rami.

Steve approached Emersyn, leaning down, and gave her a chaste kiss. "I missed you this morning," he whispered against the shell of her ear. "My bed's too cold without you."

Oliver, within earshot, rolled his eyes, and jutted out his lip in a pout. "Why can't I find my sexy rock star?"

Emersyn laughed, looping her arm in Oliver's as they followed the charge into the school.

Entering the drama room, Garrett and Dee were sitting on the choir bleachers locked in what looked like an intense conversation. With surprise, Dee got to her feet, Garrett following, her eyes wide as she took them all in.

"I called in the troops." Garrett said, giving everyone a grateful smile, his gaze settling on Jaxon as he added. "With Jaxon's help, of course."

Dee looked up at Jaxon, with so much love and adoration in her eyes, and Emersyn felt her breath catch as she watched her friend run into the arms of the man she loved. A painful lump constricted her throat as Dee let all her emotions out in a crashing wave of tears against Jaxon's chest. She looked up at Steve, whose face was full of empathy, and he put his arm around her protectively, pulling her to his side. Everyone stepped forward, surrounding Dee with their support and reassuring her it would be okay.

"We're going to rebuild these sets and make them even better," a man wearing a Hastings Hardware T-shirt said with determination, which elicited cheers from everyone, including herself, and they followed the man down the stairs to the gymnasium. Immediately, the man she now had figured out was Hayden Hastings, the owner of the Hardware store on Main Street, set to work delegating tasks when an angry voice echoed through the expansive space.

Hayden turned around to find a very angry Anders charging over to the crew, fists clenched, ready for a fight.

"Here we go." Steve whispered just loud enough for her to hear.

A handful of the men from their crew stepped forward, flagging Hayden as Anders confronted them, his face beet red and eyes bursting with flames. "You guys can't be here!" he yelled. "School is over, and you aren't authorized!"

"We have permission from the principal." Hayden said calmly, not wanting to get Anders more riled up than he already was.

"I don't care what you have, get out, all of you losers!" he yelled, pointing to the door.

"Seriously, calm down, man." Davis said, stepping in line with Hayden, his arms crossed over his muscular chest. "We're here for Dee to rebuild these sets."

Anders let out what could only be described as a maniacal laugh and started pacing, obviously on agitation overload. He turned back to both Hayden and Davis, getting within a foot of their faces. "This is my gym, and you don't have a right to be in it. This fucking musical is stupid anyway, so get out before I kick you out!" he yelled again.

Hayden was about to reply when Dee stormed past the entire crew and got within inches of Anders before Jaxon pulled Dee back and stepped in front of her protectively.

Steve looked down at Emersyn, and pulled her tightly to his side, whispering, "This guy is unpredictable; stay close."

Jaxon got into Anders face and said calmly, "We have every right to be here."

"The hell you do." Anders spat out. "This is outside the agreed-upon time for this idiotic production. Without your sets, this whole thing is done."

"We're here to rebuild them." Hayden reiterated, flagging Jaxon.

Anders stepped back and let out a huge guffaw. "Rebuild them? Fantastic more batting practice for me!" he said, mimicking the swinging of a baseball bat.

"Bingo," Steve whispered. "Proof. Keep talking, you idiot."

Emersyn glanced to the side of the barricade of men and saw Garrett standing there with his phone in the air recording the entire confrontation. *Yes!*

"At least one of us can still hit a target. Poor ex-baseball player, never quite good enough for the big leagues." Anders taunted before letting out another insane laugh.

The wall of men stepped forward, crowding Anders and Emersyn couldn't see beyond them, but she could hear Anders' words clear as day.

"Needed your army, I see." he growled as the men pressed forward. "Can't fight your own battles, old man?" he laughed, his tone nasty and full of disdain. "I don't know why you bother with Dee; she will open those legs for anyone."

Burning heat rose to Emersyn's face as anger took over and she stepped forward wanting to defend her friend, but Steve gripped her tightly to hold her back. Her eyes flitted over to Dee, her face full of hurt and anger.

"Whoa, that's way over the line." Garrett said, making Emersyn's eyes dart over to him. "And I believe Principal Parker will agree with me, Anders."

The entire crew murmured in agreement and turned back to the altercation. "That's entrapment!" Anders yelled, his voice cracking. "You can't record me without my permission. That's illegal!"

A man who looked a lot like Jaxon, but bulkier with longer wavy hair, stepped forward. "Actually, he can." he replied as he pulled something out of his pocket.

Savanah leaned into Emersyn. "That's Jaxon's brother, Cade."

"I'm an RCMP officer, and he is well within his rights under the Canadian Evidence Act." Cade said calmly as he flashed him something, pulled out his phone and seemed to be having a conversation with someone on the line. Emersyn couldn't make out what he was saying, so she looked up at Steve.

"He's calling for backup," he said, letting out a long exhale as Cade ended the call and put his phone and what Emersyn now assumed was a badge back in his pocket.

"Come with me, Mr. Barick. You show me where that

bat is, and you're going to come with me to the station. Go willingly, and I won't have to use these." Cade said, holding up something metal and shiny. *Handcuffs.*

Emersyn wrapped her arms around Steve in a reassuring hug as Dee, tears cascading down her face, raced past them, disappearing into the drama room.

Savanah went to follow her, but Rami pulled her back and shook his head. "Let Jaxon talk to her."

Jaxon disappeared into the drama room, and Steve held Emersyn tightly against him as Garrett approached, waving his phone in the air, an accomplished smile on his face.

"Got the entire thing and will be bringing this to administration in the morning. Even without Anders' little tantrum, I believe vandalism charges are grounds for dismissal."

Everyone praised his quick thinking as Hayden approached, his face flushed after the altercation. He let out a long exhale and clapped Garrett on the back. "Great job, man! Now that that's over, let's get to work and do this for Dee."

* * *

It was late, and Steve leaned against the wall, looking as exhausted as the rest of the crew. He glanced over at Emersyn, who was huddled close with Dee, their gazes on Oliver very obviously flirting with Owen Isley. *Interesting.*

Looking around at the newly built sets, the scent of sawdust and paint in the air, accomplishment bloomed in his chest as he took in what remained of the construction crew, most of the originals still there, cleaning up the sawdust and scraps of wood. He pushed off the wall, reaching for the last of the empty paint cans that he gathered and walked them over to the others by the gym door. Jaxon approached him and clapped him on the shoulder with appreciation.

"Thanks for all your help, Steve," he said, with gratitude. "If you and Emersyn want to head home, go ahead. We're almost done here."

Steve nodded and thanked Jaxon as he made his way to his girl. He wrapped his arms around her from behind, and Dee surveyed them with an adoring smile. "I love all of this." She gestured between Steve and Emersyn as she walked off to find Jaxon.

Emersyn turned, going on her tiptoes to loop her arms around his neck.

"Do you want to come home with me tonight?" he asked, lifting her off her feet.

She nodded. "There's no place I'd rather be.

Steve smiled, kissing her chastely, wishing he could have her with him every night. Her in his bed, curled up against him and waking with her every morning, simply felt right. Like it was exactly where she was meant to be. Perhaps what he had planned for them this weekend would give him the answers he needed to make it a reality.

CHAPTER 11

They drove east, the tall evergreens shading the highway as the sun was starting to set. Emersyn looked out the window, watching as the wall of evergreens turned to patterned walls of rock, with random inukshuks dotting their cliffs. She turned to face Steve; her brows drawn together.

"You know when you said you wanted to take me away for the weekend, I was thinking maybe a nice hotel or a charming bed-and-breakfast. I didn't think you would take me into the woods literally. If you haven't figured it out yet, Steve, I'm not exactly a roughing-it kind of girl," she informed, glancing out the window again, wariness in her tone.

"This is a place my parents have brought Raya and I many times," he said as he turned down a gravel road taking them deeper into the trees. "Trust me, I think you'll like this more than you think."

Emersyn drew quiet a moment then asked, "You're actually a serial killer, right? Going to kill me and feed me to a bear or something," she said, her voice dripping with sarcasm and a hint of suspicion.

Steve simply laughed and reached for her hand, giving it a reassuring squeeze. "Stop thinking the worst and keep an open mind."

They drove past a sign that said Wilders Hideaway, and Emersyn fidgeted in her seat uncomfortably. Steve could feel the apprehension oozing off her as they neared their destination, and he knew he had chosen right. This test of their relationship would be risky, and this entire weekend was going to pull her out of her comfort zone, but it was a risk he was willing to take to get her to finally talk. She needed to learn to trust him fully, and out here in the middle of nowhere, far from what she considered safe, she had no other choice.

They pulled up to what looked like a large tent on a platform, the front open and exposed to the elements. "This is a Prospector Tent and our home away from home for the weekend."

* * *

EMERSYN LET her lids fall closed, praying to the powers that be, that this was just a bad dream she was about to wake from. Her eyes slowly opened, the tent still there and not miraculously replaced by a posh hotel. Disappointingly turning her gaze to Steve, she gave him an "are you kidding me" look as she asked, "You're not serious?"

"Dead serious," he replied with a smirk, opening his door and getting out of his vehicle. She hesitantly followed, slowly meeting him in front of the tent. The tent was a wooden structure with two large logs criss-crossed in the front, obviously holding the tent's shape. It was more rounded like a dome than a tent with sharper edges, but it didn't have a wall on the end, leaving it open to the outdoors. Steve reached for her hand and led her up the stairs to the platform and inside, flicking on solar-powered lights to illuminate the tent. Scanning the space, Emersyn found a wooden table for four on one side, a set of bunk beds against the back makeshift wall and a double-wide futon against the other wall. Just outside the open entrance, was a small propane cooktop on what appeared to be an outdoor kitchenette. Two colorful Adirondack chairs sat out on the narrow deck for lounging and stargazing. It was rustic, and for those that loved to camp and enjoy the outdoors, this tent was prob-ably a luxury, but to Emersyn, it was her worst nightmare. "Cozy, right?" Steve asked enthusiastically, his eyes twin-kling in the glow of the solar lights.

Not answering him, her eyes darted around the space. "Where's the washroom?" She asked, horrified to not see a separate room.

As if reading her mind, he answered, "Just behind the tent, there's a little trail that takes you there."

"An outhouse?" She questioned, clutching her chest in horror. *If there's only an outhouse, I'm stealing his keys and driving myself back to civilization.*

"An actual independent building with a composting toilet. They're very natural and don't generally smell," he replied.

"And a shower?"

"Further down the path, there are coin-operated

showers. Don't worry, I brought lots of coins," he said, giving her a thumbs up.

Emersyn looked around, honestly considering what it would take to walk home, and immediately vetoed that idea as she was sure she would be eaten by that ravenous bear she mentioned earlier to him. She took a seat on the futon and sighed dramatically as she watched Steve bound down the steps and enthusiastically unload his vehicle, stacking coolers of food and drinks in the corner and carrying in her suitcase. He set it on the bunkbed and glanced over at her, still smiling. *Why is he fucking smiling?*

"Do you want a glass of wine and to sit out on the deck with me?" he asked, pulling a bottle of wine out of the cooler and flashing her his sexiest smile.

Why does he have to be so adorable and hot right now? She met his dark eyes, sparkling in the dim light, and put out her hand. "No need to pour me a glass, I'll take the whole bottle."

A COOL MORNING breeze rustled through the trees as Steve peeled his heavy eyelids open. The smell of fresh dirt, wet grass and evergreen fronds filled the space as a cool breeze flowed through the mosquito net wall covering the front of their tent. Breathing deeply, he stretched, then curled himself around the sleeping beauty next to him. Emersyn was so gloriously warm, and soft as she cuddled up with him on the double wide futon. After last night's dramatics and an entire bottle of wine, he was sure she was exhausted as she drifted off to sleep quickly.

Steve chuckled to himself; the memory of her aghast expression as he pulled up to the tent would forever be burned onto his brain. He couldn't help but be amused a little at her distaste over their accommodations, but he had honestly expected nothing less than her reaction. There was no question this was a stretch for Emersyn and sufficiently out of her comfort zone, and that's why he picked it. This trip alone into the woods was necessary. By pushing her to get a little uncomfortable with the hope that she would finally give him the answers he needed.

Planting kisses along her shoulder, without so much as a stir, he slipped out of bed trying not to wake her as he tucked the comforter around her to cocoon her in warmth. Rising from the bed, he stretched, feeling his tight muscles ache from sleeping on such a hard and uncomfortable surface. A futon was better than the ground, but not by much, and he could feel it this morning. Sliding on a pair of grey sweatpants, he set to work, searching the tent for what he needed. Finding a box of supplies provided by the owners of Wilders Hideaway, he pulled out a kettle, two mugs and a well-loved cast-iron frying pan. Rummaging through the contents of the coolers, he pulled out the coffee, some tea, eggs, and bacon and set to work making them breakfast. Focused on his task with his back turned towards the outdoor propane stove, he hadn't even heard Emersyn get up until he saw her traipse down the stairs and past him, towards the washroom behind the tent, with her toiletries bag in hand. No words were exchanged, she didn't even glance his way, but he could feel the cool tension radiating off her as she walked past.

Am I pushing her too far with this? Is this going to backfire on me? Will I lose her if I follow through? Too many questions floated through his mind, and although he was questioning himself and this tactic to make her talk, the only answer he could come up with was a resounding "no". He needed to do what he needed to do to get her to open up, and so far, everything was going as planned.

* * *

EMERSYN WAS ACHY, tired, hungry and had a dull, pulsing headache from too much wine the night before. The worst of it, she was still angry with Steve. She didn't want to be, but she was. He was fully aware that she wasn't an outdoorsy girl, and that she wasn't equipped for all of this fresh air and nature, and yet, he insisted on taking her here.

Frustrated, she washed her face, opting for no makeup, just lotion, and gathered her hair on top of her head, in a messy bun. *No need to look your best around here.* She brushed her teeth, put all her items back in her toiletry bag and made her way out of the bathroom, dodging a scary-looking spider web in the corner of the door frame and thankful there was no actual spider in sight. Making her way down the trail towards the tent, a loud rustling sound came from one of the trees, and her heart jolted as she clutched her toiletry bag to her chest, her eyes flitting upward. *Bears climb trees. I don't do bears. I don't do woodland creatures of any sort.* Movement caught in her peripheral vision, and her eyes darted skyward as a chittering squirrel scurried across a branch and disappeared into the foliage. She let out a long exhale, trying to steady her rapidly beating heart. *This is insane.*

Rushing back to the tent before she encountered any other wildlife, Steve was just finishing up their breakfast when she climbed the stairs to the raised tent. Putting away her bag, she took a seat at the wooden table, still trying to calm her racing heart as her eyes drifted over to Steve happily finishing up at the camp stove. He plated her meal and walked over to her, his long hair down, all shirtless and sexy, wearing low-slung grey sweatpants that left little to the imagination as to how happy he was to see her. *Why did he have to look so yummy right now?* He smiled at her saucily and leaned down to give her a kiss. She narrowed her eyes at him and made no move to bridge the gap as her protest. A smile curled his lips, and challenge flashed in his eyes as he ran his hand up the back of her neck, tangling into her hair, his fingertips massaging her scalp. *Damn you, Steve.* He knew exactly what to do to turn her into putty. He leaned in and captured her in a sensual kiss, then as quickly as he claimed her mouth he pulled away, his onyx eyes dancing with delight. "Good morning, gorgeous."

Sighing dramatically, Emersyn turned away, looking down at her breakfast and feeling her stomach rumble with a growl. He set a mug of herbal tea in front of her, and she glanced at the label on the end of the string. *English Breakfast, your favorite. He is trying. I've got to give him that.* Offering him a feigned smile, she picked up a piece of bacon, taking a bite. An involuntary moan escaped her throat, and Steve laughed, picking up his coffee and watching her intently.

"Good?" he asked, a look of mirth on his impossibly handsome face.

"It's fine." She replied, giving him the side eye and trying so hard to stand her ground but knowing she was failing miserably.

Eating their breakfast in relative silence, they did a quick cleanup, and both got dressed for the day. Steve went to his vehicle, pulling something out of the trunk, and she watched with suspicious curiosity. *Dear God, what now?* Steve returned with two pairs of hiking boots and set them down on the wooden deck with a loud thud.

"Today, we're going hiking," he announced. "There are so many amazing trails around here, and there is one lookout I would love to bring you to. The view is indescribable."

Hiking? Has he lost his ever-loving mind? Calmly, she rose from the table, walked over to the boots, scrutinizing them and gave one a light kick as she responded, "I wear size 6."

"Perfect! Raya wears size 6 ½ so I think they should work well for you," he replied, eagerness in his gaze. "It's such good exercise, and all the fresh air you breathe in today will make you sleep like a baby tonight."

Sleep. One more night closer to going home. Tricky. Hesitantly, she conceded, picking up the smaller pair of boots and taking them into the tent.

* * *

GRABBING A BACKPACK, Steve threw in a couple of water bottles, some snacks and a small first aid kit just in case they needed it. He slipped on the backpack and watched as Emersyn laced up the boots and stood from the chair, an indignant look on her face. Leading them out of the tent, he headed down a path, waiting for her to come into step with him. Putting out his hand, she reluctantly took it, offering him a squinted side-eye. Taking a deep breath, it wasn't lost on Steve how frustrated she was with him. It pained him to do this to her, but it was now or never. *Stay the course, and you'll get your answers.*

Walking together down the path that wound through the trees, it started to narrow, forcing them to walk single file. Letting Emersyn go ahead of him, she carefully walked over fallen tree branches, and large tree roots that had pushed their way out of the ground in twisted curves. The forest was thick and dense, but Emersyn led the way, and for a moment Steve wondered if she was enjoying getting lost with him in the woods. Having walked for a good hour, they slowly made their way upward, the trail sloping and rocky, leading to the lookout.

The sound of a rustling in a bush close to the path made them both stop, Emersyn instinctively gravitating closer to him, her eyes wide and cautious as a deer appeared several feet away and raised its head to stare at them. The majestic doe was curious but not bothered by their presence. Emersyn held her hand to her chest, let out a long exhale, and turned to continue down the trail but caught her foot on a jagged rock and stumbled forward, causing her to fall hard on the rocky path.

"Are you okay?" Steve asked with concern as he knelt beside her, trying to meet her eyes. Her forehead was scrunched up and her eyes glossy as she held back tears.

Guilt consumed him as he checked her over and dusted off her knees, which had taken the brunt of the fall. "No cuts or scrapes," he said reassuringly, searching her stormy eyes.

Turning to sit on her behind, she rubbed her hands together to brush off the dirt and gravel that had embedded into her skin. She didn't reply, nary a word said as her breaths came out heavy and she stared at her hands, imprinted by the gravel from the trail.

"Are you okay?" he asked again, attempting to meet her dodgy gaze.

Emersyn slowly raised her eyes to him, daggers shooting from their depths as she enunciated each word, "I am not fucking okay."

"Are you mad?" he asked, taking a seat next to her.

"Do you think?" she asked, squinting at him.

"Good, I want you to be mad," he volleyed, getting to his feet and putting out his hand to her.

"Why would you want that?" she asked as she took his hand to help her up. She brushed the dirt from the back of her shorts and glared at him as she asked. "Is that what this whole awful trip is about? Cornering me so I will talk. Fuck you, Steve."

"If that's what it takes, yes. That was my plan." He answered truthfully. "You only give me bits and pieces and refuse to completely open to me. You say you trust me, but I don't think you do fully; otherwise, I wouldn't have to resort to something like this to get you stripped down of your defences, so you'll finally talk to me. I love you, want you to be a part of my life, and I think I've earned and deserve your trust."

Emersyn slowly blinked, her body tensing as she met his impenetrable stare. Letting out an exasperated huff, she pushed past him and set back down the way they came. "I want you to take me home, Steve! I'm not spending another moment on this godforsaken trail. Not another minute having you try to fix me and mold me into this perfect girl who doesn't have any problems. Someone who doesn't have a mother who controls her whole world."

"That's not fair, Em," he said, reaching for her arm to halt her. She swung around, her hands on hips, her eyes breathing fire. "I love you just as you are, cracked, bruised, fractured or however you want to refer to yourself as. But you keep saying your mom controls you, and I've been trying to get my head around that. I can't understand if she is so terrible to you, why she is still a part of your life. You're 27 years old, Em. Don't you think it's time to stand up to her and make a clean break?"

Emersyn looked away and let out a long-exasperated exhale. "It's not that simple, Steve. I wish it was, but it's not."

"Then help me to understand why!" he exclaimed. "Why won't you stand up to her and take back control. You're deserving of way more than what she gives you. You just need to make a choice to walk away. Because that's what I see. I see someone that is so scared to break away that she would rather live half a life than live her life fully and pursue her dreams."

"Fuck you, Steve! You don't get it. I can't!" she yelled back, hurt and anger in her tone.

"Why not? Please Em, help me to understand!" he pleaded.

She turned again, making her way back down the path until he caught up to her, putting his hand on her shoulder, making her stop in her tracks.

"Leave me alone." She said, her voice cracking with emotion.

"No, I won't," he said, spinning her around to face him and meeting her eyes with all the sincerity he could muster. "I love you, Em, and if your mother is going to control you and your life, it's going to affect our relationship, eventually. I need to know now and prepare myself for how that's going to affect us. Before I plan a future with you. Because I want that. I want to be with you forever, Em. I love you that much."

Her eyes welled up with frustrated tears as he fixed his gaze on her, and he could see her trying to process what he had just said to her. Bridging the gap between them, he cupped her face with his hands as he whispered, "Help me to understand, baby."

She shoved him away, breaking his hold and turning away from him as she whispered. "Fuck you."

Steve ran his hands over his face, feeling completely vexed by the stubborn woman before him. Letting out an exhale, he knew he couldn't give up. Not now, not after they had come this far. Their future depended on this, and she was worth fighting for.

"Em, you can push me away, but it's not going to change how I feel about you. I want you to be part of my future, and honestly, I deserve an explanation." He added, Emersyn unmoving. Heat rose to his face, his frustration with her peaking as he blurted out, "Em, for fucks sake, speak to me!"

She whirled around, flames in her eyes as she rasped out. "I'm so mad!"

"Good! Get mad! Get so damn mad that you finally start living your life for you and not her."

"You don't understand; I can't get away from my mom, even if I want to." She let out an aggravated growl. "I am so angry at her for that, I hate her for that!"

"Why can't you get away? Tell me!" he urged, cautiously drawing closer and pressing her to explain.

"Because she's sick, Steve! Because my mother is 54 years old and is in a retirement home! Because she has Alzheimer's, and she doesn't even know who I am most days, and because I'm all she has. She has no family, no friends, only me. And every day, I feel guilty because I'm so damn angry at her for being sick. I'm so angry that after I finally pulled away from her, after I finally was starting to live my own life, my own way, she managed to pull me back in. I'm angry that despite the bullying and abuse, I still love her. I'm angry that she gets to forget all the bad memories she created for me, and I'm forced to relive them every day. I'm mad that now I deal with anxiety and depression, and when I look in the mirror, all I see is her. And you know what makes me the angriest? That I could have what she has. I could carry that awful disease within me, and I could pass it on to my child someday. I'm just so fucking angry, Steve! I don't want to be this angry! I don't want to feel this way!"

Her mother has Alzheimer's. Eyes glazed over with compassionate tears, Steve suggested, "Scream. Scream out that anger. That fear. That frustration right here in these woods. No one is here to judge you. I'll even scream with you if you want." Emersyn hesitated, her eyes flashing fire. "Go on! Scream as loud as you can."

Seeing the apprehension in her anguished expression, she looked up to the sky, so blue between the trees, opened her mouth, took a deep breath in and let out a wail so piercing and painful, his breath caught, and his heart shattered. Emersyn closed her eyes tight as a dam of tears broke through her long lashes, trailed down her face and she crumpled to the ground. There to catch her fall, Steve gathered her into his arms, as she sobbed into his chest. He stroked her hair lovingly, his mind reeling at what had just transpired. Her mother was sick, and now knowing the truth, it explained so much. Emersyn literally had no one, and the one person who she did have was slowly having her memories erased. Her mother was slowly forgetting her, and he couldn't fathom how she was managing all of this on her own.

Scooping her into his arms, he rose to his feet and climbed up the trail, knowing the lookout was close. When they reached the pinnacle, he set her down on the observation bench and put his arm around her, pulling her close. As they took in the spectacular view of the lake and the gorgeous greens and browns of the dense forest before them, Emersyn wiped the tears from her face with her palms as she clung to him, her grip tight. A cool crisp breeze kissed their faces as they sat in silence, and the realization that a tide had turned in these woods washed over them. A crushing weight had been lifted, and they were finally able to breathe.

* * *

EMERSYN CURLED up on Steve's lap as he sat in the Adirondack chair nursing a beer. She reached for the long neck of the beer bottle and took a swig, making him grin as she handed it back to him. The night sky was perfectly clear, and a blanket of incandescent stars shone brightly above them. She had never seen so many stars before. It felt like the entire universe was laid out just for them, and she had to admit it was probably one of the most beautiful things she had ever seen in her life. Languidly, Steve trailed his fingertips over the exposed skin of her neck, making goosebumps rise with his gentle touch, and she sighed contentedly.

"I want you to know, you're not alone," he said, breaking them from their quiet reverie. "Whatever you need me to do to help you with your mom. I'm ready and willing to help." Glancing up at him, she searched his eyes, only to see sincerity in their depths. "I mean it, Em. I want to help. If you want me to come with you when you visit her, if you want or need help covering the costs of her care, I'll help whatever way I can if you will let me."

This man. Emotion bloomed in her chest with his words as she cupped his face and kissed him deeply, feeling the love between them burn strong. Pulling away, she met his benevolent gaze as she said, "Steve, you are the most selfless person I have ever met. I love you so much."

"I love you too," he said, curling his large hand around the back of her neck and capturing her lips with a passionate kiss. Melting into his embrace, he rose from the chair, cradling her in his arms as he carried her inside the tent. Setting her next to the futon, he undressed them slowly, taking time to kiss and caress each part of her body he exposed, as he laid her out and took a moment to stare at her with reverence. "I have never seen anyone look more beautiful." He declared, his voice weighted with emotion and ardor. Taking in her fill of him as well, she wanted to memorize this moment, her impossibly handsome boyfriend, silhouetted against the light of the moon.

"Make love to me," she whispered, her eyes meeting his, as her body heated with desire.

A coquettish smile tugged at his lips as he covered her, the weight of his body pressing her into the mattress of the futon. The pulse in her core was strong, and as he settled at her juncture, his body hard and ready as he teased her soft folds, preparing them both. Holding himself above her, his eyes intense and hungry, he held her gaze as their bodies came together. Every time with Steve, new and ardent, each sensation heightened by their growing connection. It was like their bodies were meant for each other, the yin to the other's yang. Connected physically, emotionally, spiritually. As they moved together, climbing closer to the pinnacle, she was certain that this was who she wanted to spend the rest of her life with and when they found their release together; she knew beyond a shadow of a doubt that Steve was her forever.

CHAPTER 12

It was Spring Musical Week, and as Steve and Emersyn walked into the Primrose High School you could literally feel the palpable excitement in the air. They had one more practice before the dress rehearsal tomorrow, and with Anders out of their way, there would be no interruptions as they helped these students perfect their performances.

Steve took his place at the piano as Dee approached them looking both gratified and melancholy.

"Are you excited it's almost over?" Emersyn asked, putting her arm around her friend. "Dee, you have done an incredible job."

Dee gave her a grateful look as her gaze drifted over to Steve. "I am but a little sad too. I honestly can't thank you both enough for everything you two did to make this musical happen." She said, her voice edged with emotion.

Rising from the piano, Steve strode over and both Emersyn and Steve wrapped her in a hug. Another body crashed their group hug, and Oliver was there smiling brightly at all of them. "Can't have a group hug without me," he declared, giving them all a squeeze.

The gym doors opened, and as Dee walked off to greet her cast, Emersyn curled her arm around Steve's waist. *If it weren't for this production, if it weren't for me agreeing to help a friend, I never would have reconnected with Steve and fallen in love.* She glanced up at Steve, meeting his fervent gaze as mutual gratitude passed between them, both knowing that their lives had been forever changed by this experience.

Steve's cell phone buzzed, and Emersyn's vibrated in her pocket. Oliver walked over to them, holding his phone in his hand. Her eyes flitted between them as she swiped open her phone and clicked on her texts. With widening eyes, she looked from Oliver to Steve, smiles on their faces too as they read the group text silently together:

Jaxon Isley: Hey there, Dream Team! I plan to ask Dee to marry me tomorrow at the dress rehearsal, and I need your help. Can I count on you?

* * *

THE GYMNASIUM WAS FULL, students and staff chattering loudly, the sounds of their voices echoing against the walls of the expansive space. Steve took a seat at the piano, Emersyn in his eyeline as she sat next to Oliver, their heads together in conversation. Capturing his gaze, he gave Emersyn a sly thumbs up, making her grin brightly.

Dee entered the gym and stepped to the microphone

as everyone in the gym noisily took their seats and the teachers attempted to quiet down their students. "Hello everyone!" she greeted; her smile wide as she beamed with excitement. "You all have the privilege of being the first in Primrose to see our production of the award-winning musical *Singin' in the Rain*. Your students and classmates have worked hard on this production, and I hope you love it as much as we do. So, without further ado, we present to you *Singin' in the Rain*." Dee took her seat next to Emersyn in the front row and her eyes met Steve's, as she gave him a nod to start. He started to play as the lights dimmed and the curtains opened to a projection screen showing the opening sequence that started the show.

The next two hours flew by. Steve played and watched in wonder at what the students had accomplished. A deep swell of pride rose in his chest at being part of this experience as he glanced at Dee, Emersyn and Oliver, their eyes fixed on the stage. Dee had done it. Her vision, their teamwork along with the student's dedication, all evident in the reaction of the enraptured audience. As the final number ended and the curtain closed, he glanced at Emersyn and Oliver, both staring at him with knowing grins. *You're up. This is Dee and Jaxon's moment.* The curtain reopened, and he started to play the love song from the play, "You Were Meant for Me."

Jaxon appeared on stage, spotlight on him, standing alone in front of the microphone, dressed like Gene Kelly in his 1940s garb and looking every bit the movie star himself.

Steve glanced at Dee, whose midnight eyes were wide

and her mouth agape as Jaxon stepped to the microphone and spoke. "I have a special song I want to sing for a very special woman. Someone I love very much, and I know was meant for me." Then he started to sing, his rich voice filling the room. *Wow, he's pretty good.* Steve's eyes flitted over to Emersyn who gave him a wide smile and a surprised shrug. Jaxon finished the song, and Steve continued to play the melody softly as Jaxon asked, "Could Ms. Jones, please come up to the stage?"

He watched as Emersyn gave her a gesture to go, and Oliver leaned in whispering to her. Dee hesitantly rose to her feet and disappeared through the side door of the stage. She reappeared on stage, walking past her cast waiting in the wings and joined Jaxon on stage. He took her hands, and although Steve couldn't make out exactly what he said, he could see the emotion in Dee's eyes, and his heart swelled for his friend. Looking towards Emersyn, who was clutching Oliver's hand, her other hand over her heart, he smiled. Jaxon dropped to one knee, pulled out a ring box and presented it to Dee as her eyes sparkled and he could make out the gleam of happy tears from his perch on the piano bench. Suddenly, a loud "YES!" echoed through the large space followed by a "YES, I will marry you!"

The entire gym erupted, and he looked to the audience that was laughing, hugging, crying, their eyes fixed on the newly engaged couple embracing on the stage. Steve glanced at Emersyn, whose eyes were fixed on his, and he knew. His heart was certain at that moment that Emersyn Bridger would one day say "yes" to him too.

* * *

THE WEEK FLEW BY. Three fantastic performances of *Singin' in the Rain* graced the Primrose stage, and as the final curtain fell, Emersyn couldn't help but feel a deep sadness that it was all over. Having been part of a production like this, made her think that maybe there was more for her out there. She thought about all the productions she had been a part of over the years and smiled at the fond memories. Perhaps she needed to take Dee's path and consider teaching herself. The sheer pleasure it was to work with the students and their eagerness to learn made her radiate with pride. Would she teach at a school or perhaps somewhere else? Surely there were jobs out there that could use her level of expertise. So many possibilities ran through her head, and for the first time in a long time, she was excited to see what the future held.

Steve found her after the last performance and pulled her in for a hug, planting a kiss on her head. "Well, that's a wrap. Kind of sad that it's over."

"Me too." She said, jutting out her lip. "It's really got me thinking about what I might want to do in the future."

"Does that future include me?" he asked with a cocked an eyebrow as he grinned down at her.

"Of course." She replied, smiling at him dreamily.

"Then I'll support you in whatever it is you want to do," he declared, lifting her chin, and lowering his lips to hers for a tender kiss.

Gratitude filled Emersyn's heart as she curled her arms around Steve's neck and he lifted her into his arms. So much had changed in only a few short months.

Knowing that the reality of her life was out in the open now and that she had something to aspire to career-wise, Emersyn was ready to look to the future. A future with the man she loved.

* * *

PULLING into Layne and Juli's yard, cheery bright balloons greeted them as they found a parking spot. The driveway was full, and immediately Steve's eyes scanned for Rex's truck, not sure if he was coming to this celebration or not.

"Is that the infamous garage studio? The place that started it all?" Emersyn asked, pointing to the double-wide detached garage to the side of the house.

"It is!" he replied with a wistful smile. "I miss the garage sometimes. So many amazing memories there."

Retrieving their gift from the back seat, he handed it to Emersyn as he took her hand, and they walked around the house to the backyard where the birthday celebration was well underway. There were adults milling around the yard and deck and kids running wild to and from the brightly colored bouncy house in the middle of the expansive backyard. The delicious smell of burgers and hotdogs on the grill wafted through the air and made him immediately hungry. Layne, donning a #1 Dad baseball cap and a grilling apron that said, "Don't worry, I watched a YouTube Video" spotted them as they approached.

"Hey Steve and Em! Glad you could make it!" he said as he flipped a burger. "The birthday girl is in the bouncy house if you want to say hi!"

Emersyn gave Steve an excited look as she carried the

large gift bag stuffed to the brim with gifts and a copious amount of colorful tissue paper. When they shopped together for the gifts, Emersyn had explained that she had never been to a kid's birthday party before. Steve couldn't fathom that, as with his large family alone, birthday celebrations were a weekly norm when he was a kid. Because of this, he simply watched as she excitedly picked out toys and clothes for Layne and Juli's three-year-old daughter, Tabitha, and smiled with each aww and "isn't this darling".

As they approached the bouncy house, the sweet, familiar giggle sounded from inside as the birthday girl herself, with big brown eyes and bouncy pigtails, appeared by the entrance. She was bouncing with her older cousins and, as always, she made Steve's heart swell at the sight of her adorable face.

"There's the birthday girl!" he exclaimed, putting out his arms to her.

Tabitha stopped bouncing, and her smile grew big as she jumped into his waiting arms. "Uncle Steve!" she squealed; her face flushed red and sweaty from exertion.

He turned Tabitha to face Emersyn, and her eyes were curious as she eyed Emersyn timidly, informing, "Uncle Steve, it's my burfday."

"I know Tabs! And how old are you today?" he asked, tapping his chin. "Let me guess, 22, or maybe 66."

Tabitha slapped him playfully on the chest with her little hand and threw her head back with a melodic giggle. "No, Uncle Steve, I'm this many," she said, holding up three chubby little fingers.

"Oh, three!" he exclaimed, tickling her sides and making her squirm and giggle. Tabitha stopped and looked over to Emersyn, meeting her gaze with a shy smile as Steve said, "This is my girlfriend, Emersyn."

Tabitha analyzed her for a moment, a sweet smile curling her cupid's bow lips, as she wiggled herself free from his hold. Steve set her down, and Emersyn crouched down, putting her hand out to Tabitha.

"Hi, happy birthday." She said. "We have a present for you."

Tabitha's shy smile turned bright and wide as she took in the colorful gift bag that was larger than her.

"Danke." she said happily, then without any hesitation walked into Emersyn's arms and looped her chubby little arms around her neck in a big hug. Emersyn looked up at Steve, her expression a mix of surprise and wonder as Tabitha clung to her like a koala bear.

Emersyn rose to her feet, carrying Tabitha in her arms, and they walked over to the deck where most of the adults were gathered. Tabitha played with a ringlet of Emersyn's hair, twirling it around her finger as she smiled at her sweetly with her big brown eyes transfixed on her.

"Tabs, I see you've found a new friend." Juli said as she approached. "You must be Emersyn." Juli greeted, putting out her hand. "I'm Layne's wife, Juli."

The women greeted each other as Savanah joined them, and they pulled Emersyn, still holding Tabitha, away into the house.

"You probably won't see her for a while," Rami said, reaching into a cooler and producing an ice-cold beer.

Steve laughed, unscrewed the cap, and nabbed a patio chair next to him. The men clinked their beers and settled back against their chairs.

Rami leaned into Steve, his voice low and eyes playful. "I'm liking this whole thing with you and Em. She's feisty, and I think she challenges you. I must admit it's kind of fun to watch."

"Oh, did I need a challenge?" Steve asked with a deep chuckle.

"I think so. I mean, you're such an even-keel guy, Steve. Always quiet and unassuming, preferring to be in the background and let others take the spotlight." Steve nodded, agreeing with his description. "Em, on the other hand, is the spotlight. She has 'star' written all over her. You're kind of the perfect partnership. You're willing to let her shine, and she challenges you to put yourself out there more."

Steve looked at Rami and knew he had hit the nail on the head. Even though some would consider them opposites, it was their differences that made them work. They balanced each other out.

Layne came over with a tray of meat fresh off the grill and set it on the table. He pulled out his phone, swiping it open, then shoved it back into his pocket, unease on his face as he asked. "Has anyone heard from Rex? I messaged him earlier in the week to remind him about the party, and he hasn't responded to me."

Steve's brows furrowed as guilt hung like a veil over him. "I haven't talked to him in a few weeks. I've been too preoccupied with the musical and with Em."

Rami shook his head. "I haven't seen or heard from him in a while either."

"Did any of you notice his strange behavior at the last studio session? He's always high energy, and he passed out cold after the last song. Also, his eyes were red, and pupils dilated." Steve said, deep concern edging his voice.

"He definitely wasn't his usual self and hasn't been for a while," Rami agreed. "I thought maybe he'd been out too late at the bar or something, but from the look of him, it seems there's more at play here. There must be. Do you know anything about this Charlene he's been hanging out with?"

Steve ran his hand over his face, tension and worry rising in his chest. "When they first got together, I heard some rumors, which I addressed with Rex, but he said she wasn't hanging out with him anymore."

"Who?" Rami asked, leaning in further, his brows furrowed in question.

"I can't remember his name, but she used to date a well-known drug dealer in St. Augustine. I heard he got busted, did some time, but I have no idea where he is now. For all I know, he's still locked up. I honestly don't know much about him."

"Or who he was associated with." Rami added, looking up at Layne then back down to Steve, worry etched on his face.

"This isn't good, guys." Layne said, shaking his head. "Rex may be a foul-mouthed oaf sometimes, but he's a good guy at heart. He adores Tabs and would never miss her party."

They all nodded, deep unease on their faces as they discussed what to do with their bandmate and how they were going to confront him.

* * *

THE PARTY WAS WINDING DOWN. The grandparents, aunts, uncles, cousins all had gone home, leaving just the band and their significant others. The very overtired and over-sugared birthday girl had been tucked into bed as the sun was starting to set on the horizon. Emersyn curled up on Steve's lap, finding her comfortable spot and letting out a contented sigh. Today had been fun, and she truly felt like she had found her tribe. Savanah and Juli had welcomed her like she was a sister, and of course the guys had made her feel like one of their family. What Steve had here was something incredibly special, and Emersyn was honored to be brought into their fold.

Juli slid open the patio door and joined them on the deck, letting out a long-exhausted exhale. "Tabitha is finally asleep."

Layne put his arm around his wife, pulled her in close and planted an affectionate kiss on her temple.

Savanah was curled up with Rami, and it was evident everyone was well fed, and quickly reaching a comatose state.

Steve's phone buzzed in his pocket, disrupting the quiet calm, and he pulled it out quickly to turn it off. As he swiped open the phone, his brows furrowed, and his body tensed. Emersyn glanced over at the caller ID on his screen.

"It's Rex's dad," Steve said, everyone sitting up straight and leaning in as he called him back and put his phone on speaker.

"Steve, Rex was brought into St. Augustine General. Can you come to the hospital?"

All the color drained from Steve's face as he said, "The guys are all here. We're on our way."

Steve lifted Emersyn off his lap and stood, the men following. "I'm coming with you." Emersyn said.

"Me too." Savanah piped in as they sprinted to their vehicles. Juli gave Layne a quick hug, deep concern on her face as he got into Steve's vehicle, and they raced off the yard towards St. Augustine.

CHAPTER 13

*P*ulling up at St. Augustine General Hospital, they all got out and rushed towards the emergency room entrance. Mr. and Mrs. Johnson were at the check-in desk, and Mr. Johnson was consoling his crying wife.

"Rex, where is he?" Steve asked, his pulse racing as he surveyed his parents and the worst-case scenario flashed through his head.

"He's in surgery right now. He was beaten up badly and had a seizure as they brought him in." Rex's father informed as he pulled his wife tighter to him, her face buried in his shoulder as her body shook with sobs.

Steve ran his hand over his face, his heart jackhammering in his chest. "What happened?"

Sylvio Conti, the owner of the Pickled Pig, walked up behind them and gestured to Rex's dad that he would fill the guys in. They followed him into the waiting room, finding a quiet corner.

"What happened to Rex?" Rami asked impatiently.

"It looks like a drug deal gone bad," Sylvio said, shaking his head. "We had just opened the bar, and I noticed a bag of garbage had not been taken out, so I went to put it into the dumpster when I heard a groan. I walked around the side of the dumpster, and Rex was lying there on the ground, his face swollen and bloody, and I thought maybe he had been stabbed, but I quickly checked him over and there were no wounds. They kicked the shit out of him though as he was in bad shape."

"Fuck," Steve growled out. "Who did it?"

"No idea exactly, but I have my suspicions. This guy who used to frequent St. Augustine and got nailed with drug possession a few years back, recently got out of jail, and I saw him come into the bar a few times. I've had my eye on him, watching him like a hawk, knowing his reputation. I even had a meeting with my staff to tell me if they see anything fishy going down and to let me know immediately. But so far, nothing. With this happening to Rex, I'm now wondering if he was conducting some transactions in the parking lot, maybe just off the property. I'm not sure. Security hasn't seen anything, but I don't have security at the back of the building, just cameras. I'll be bringing the footage to the RCMP tonight after close."

"This guy you mentioned, was he associated with Charlene in any way? You know that redhead Rex has been hanging around lately?" Layne asked.

"Yeah, from what I remember, they used to be quite serious. She had her addictions too, but she seemed to get clean after he was thrown in the clink. I did, however, see her the other night hanging out at a table with a few of his friends. I didn't see him though." Sylvio answered, worry etched on his expression.

"Geez," Layne said, running his hand over his face. "I had a gut feeling something was wrong with that girl."

Sylvio shook his head. "I'm not going to sugar coat it guys, it was pretty bad. He was barely conscious when I found him, and then he had a seizure in the ambulance. He apparently had a lot of substance in his system from what I overheard."

"Damn it. Why didn't I confront him earlier?" Steve exclaimed, getting up from his seat and pacing back and forth.

"Don't blame yourself, Steve. People dealing with addiction are really good at hiding things if they want to." Sylvio explained, looking up at him.

"But I'm his closest friend. And I suspected something wasn't right with him. I should've said something. Fuck." Steve cursed, turning and clenching his fists.

Rami and Layne rose from their seats and put their hands on Steve's shoulders. "We all should have spoken up." Layne added, trying to meet his gaze.

"What matters right now is that Rex comes out of this and gets help." Rami said. "And we'll stand by him as he does.

* * *

EMERSYN CAME BACK from the vending machine and handed a soda to Steve. He had been alternating between sitting and pacing all night, and they were still waiting for word about Rex and his condition. Mr. and Mrs. Johnson sat huddled together in a corner and were joined by Rex's two younger sisters, who were holding hands so tightly their knuckles were white as their gazes remained downcast. A doctor came out of the sliding door, causing them all to look up. He leaned towards the nurse at the front desk, and she pointed over to the family gathered in the waiting room. He strode over, his face serious and mouth in a grim line.

"Family of Rex Johnson?" he asked, addressing Rex's parents. "Your son is out of surgery, and we were able to stop the internal bleeding. At the moment he's stable. I would like to pull you into a private room to discuss his condition further, if you will follow me."

They nodded and stood up, following the doctor while his bandmates watched warily as they were taken into a private room off the main emergency area.

"What do you think they're discussing?" Savanah asked, looking between each of the guys.

"My guess is the drugs that were in his system." Steve replied, shaking his head and running his hands through his hair. "Why didn't I say something?" Steve's voice cracked with emotion, and Emersyn put her arms around him. "I mean, I saw all the signs, and was worried, but didn't act. I was watching my best friend ruin his life, and I did nothing.

"You can't blame yourself." Rami reassured. "Rex had a choice, and he made a bad one that almost cost him his life."

Tears welled up in Steve's eyes as he blinked rapidly, and he covered his face with his hands. Emersyn's heart ached for him as she reached out to touch his arm. "Don't cry, babe. You heard the doctor; he's stable, and he's alive. You need to focus on that."

"He's like my brother, you know?" he managed between tears, as he looked up into her eyes and glanced around the room at his bandmates. "I've known him since the first day of grade one when he lent me his blue crayon." The guys all let out a little chuckle between fielding their own tears. "He was the first kid on the playground to befriend me, and he has been my ride or die ever since. For as long as I can remember, we've been friends, and I'm not sure what I would do without him."

"We get it; he's like a brother to us too." Layne said, wiping tears from his eyes. "I think we can all agree we would be lost without each other. We're family."

Steve glanced between his bandmates. Men he had been friends with for over half his life. They had all been through a lot together. They had laughed, had cried, and had confided in each other. Had been together through some extreme highs and extreme lows, and as they huddled consoling each other, he knew whatever the outcome, somehow, someway they would get through this together too.

* * *

THE CONSENSUS WAS that no member of Prairie Sound ever wanted to relive the two weeks that followed Rex's hospitalization. Rex was put into a medically induced coma to help him heal from his injuries and once he was brought out of the coma he was held at the hospital under observation until he had healed enough and undergone the initial detox so he could be put into a men's addiction facility in Winnipeg. Their upcoming album release was postponed, as was their upcoming national tour. The news that the drummer of Prairie Sound, Rex Johnson had been involved in a drug deal, was addicted to cocaine and had nearly lost his life as a result, had been splashed across social media and local news.

Despite this negative chain of events, good news did follow. The guy they suspected was to blame for Rex's beating was identified off the security tapes, and he along with several of his cronies were brought into custody with charges of drug trafficking, drug possession and assault causing bodily harm. He was immediately reincarcerated under the terms of recidivism as he had reoffended within three years of release. His friends were awaiting trial. Charlene was brought in for questioning and admitted to conspiring with her ex-boyfriend to bring him more business, which included Rex. The investigation and charges against her were pending.

EMERSYN WATCHED as Steve sat down at his piano and started to play. He had spent a lot of time at the piano over the past few weeks, and she had determined it was his way of working through his thoughts and feelings regarding Rex. Music his therapy.

She tossed in the ramen noodles into their stir-fry and mixed in the sauce. The sweet sound of "Dream a Little Dream of Me", sounded through the open space, and she smiled, remembering the first time she heard him play.

She snickered to herself, remembering how she gave him the stink eye and stuck out her tongue. *I was such a brat back then.* But she also remembered being completely mesmerized by his talent, and the way he looked at her made her feel special. If she was being honest with herself, she knew with that first meeting that she was infatuated with him, and she was pretty sure looking back that he felt the same. Something passed between them that day, something their young hearts and minds had no comprehension of, yet looking back now, it was clear an initial spark was there, all those years ago.

Turning off the burner, she covered the finished stir-fry with a lid and set down two plates, utensils and filled their glasses with water. Steve had a pencil in his mouth and was hyper-focused on the sheet music he'd been picking away at for as long as they'd been together. She approached and slid in next to him on the bench. He took the pencil out of his mouth and wrote at the top of the sheet music, Em's Song. Her gaze flitted across the sheet music, and a smile tugged at her lips as she asked, "Is this song for me?"

Steve mirrored her smile and answered. "I started writing it after we got together, and well, I was thinking it could be your song. I mean, you could write the lyrics and maybe record it if you want to, of course," he said, meeting her questioning gaze. "I really want you to."

Emersyn glanced from Steve to the sheet music and back to Steve, tears rimming her eyes. "You mean you want to record this as our song?"

He nodded. "We're on a bit of an unexpected hiatus right now, and I spoke to our producer, you know, Sean from the day you were in the studio with us. Well, he was blown away by your voice and would love to work with you if you are down for it. I was thinking we could start with this song and, if the song writing inspiration flows, add some more."

My own songs. My voice out there in the world. Songs written with the man I love. There was only one answer to his wonderful offer.

"Yes!"

It was late and Steve still couldn't sleep. He lay curled up against Emersyn, listening to her steady breaths with his hand on her stomach. He loved how she fit just right into the groove of his body and how having her next to him made him feel complete. The recurring desire to have every night be like this, here in his home, in his bed, resurfaced, and he kissed her shoulder tenderly. She had practically moved in already and only went home once or twice during the week on days she was visiting her mother.

He pulled her deeper into the groove of his body, and she stirred, then sighed. "Your thinking woke me," she said groggily. "What's keeping you up, babe?"

He smiled and nuzzled into her neck affectionately, inhaling her sweet coconut scent. "I was just thinking how I really want you to move in here with me. You're here all the time, and it only makes sense for us to take that step."

Emersyn shifted to face him, her hands sifting through the strands of his hair, her sparkling gaze and radiant smile barely made out by the slivers of moonlight through the curtains. "Yes, I'll move in here with you."

Overjoyed, Steve leaned in and captured her lips in a searing kiss before pulling away to ask, "What about your mom?"

"I've been giving that a lot of thought actually and have already been looking into moving her here to St. Augustine. The facilities are nice here, and the cost is way less. I know she won't like it, but I think she'll get over it."

Steve caressed her face tenderly and pulled her in for another passionate kiss. Their tongues in a now familiar dance as their hands roamed over the memorized curves and edges of each other's bodies. When their desire overtook, bringing them together as one, they made love, a carnal symbol that their lives were about to intertwine forever.

CHAPTER 14

It's amazing how so much can change in a blink of an eye. Three short months after they started dating, Emersyn moved in with Steve. Everyone pitched in, including Prairie Sound, their spouses and Steve's family. Within a day, her entire world was moved from her little one-room apartment to Steve's family's historic home in downtown St. Augustine. As she stared at the wall of boxes erected in their living room, an overwhelming sense of peace washed over her and, for the first time in her life, she truly felt at home.

She turned around to see Juli and Savanah unpacking boxes labeled 'kitchen' and glanced in the spare bedroom where Layne and Rami were putting together her bed. She grabbed a few garment bags of her clothes and climbed the stairs to their loft bedroom. Steve had purchased another wardrobe for her and made room in the drawers for her things. She set to work putting away her clothes and only looked up when she noticed Steve appear on the stairs.

"Here you are," he said, carrying a box labeled shoes. "I brought you some more of your things."

She smiled as she picked up a garment bag and tossed it to the side to make room for him to set down the box.

"Be careful with those," he teased playfully. "Do you want to ruin them before you hang them up?"

She gave him a chiding look and let out a laugh as she remembered the day they picked up costumes for Dee's production. "I was so nasty to you that day."

"A little, but nothing I couldn't handle. I thought you were kind of cute," he replied, looping his arms around her. "Besides, I knew you weren't actually mad at me. You were just trying to push me away because you just couldn't handle your burning attraction to me," he dead-panned, his onyx eyes dancing with mirth.

"Oh, really?" She scoffed back with a laugh, and a playful slap to his chest. "You're so sure of that, aren't you?"

"I sure am, because I already had it bad for you, Em," he said, his tone more serious now. "I already knew that despite all your attempts to push me away, I was falling for you."

She gazed up at him through her long lashes and gave him her naughtiest look. "Do you think anyone would notice if we got busy with them downstairs?" She asked as she backed him towards the bed and gave him a little shove, making him fall to the mattress.

"I think we can do whatever we want, as this is our home," he replied with a cocked eyebrow as she crawled up the length of him and straddled his hips.

His hands slid up her t-shirt to cup her breasts, as she

leaned down and gave him a long-languid, sensual kiss, making him groan against her lips. Reaching for the button of her shorts, he unsnapped them as he slipped his hand inside to touch her where she pulsed and ached. She moaned loudly as he found her sweet spot and teased and toyed with her as she rocked unabashedly against his hand.

They could hear their friends' talking downstairs, one asking where Steve and Emersyn were and Savanah's voice saying they were upstairs as he drove her arousal higher. Suddenly the voice of Rami sounded at the bottom of the stairs, making them both pause in mid act.

"I'm going to pick up dinner at the Blue Corn. You two commence your... honestly, I don't need to know what you're doing right now, just commence."

They listened as Rami told the others that they were up there having sex and not to disturb them, which was followed by a few loud hoots and hollers.

Steve laughed as he rolled her onto her back and removed her shorts and underwear, spreading her open to him. "No more disruptions," he growled as he swiped his tongue through her sensitive folds. "Time for me to welcome you home properly."

"Hello, family!" Steve shouted as he entered his childhood home and made his way into the open kitchen and living room. He glanced outside to see his parents in the garden, and he was about to go outside to see them when Raya walked into the room, still in her pajamas and holding a pint of ice cream and a spoon.

"Hey Dork," she said, opening a drawer, taking out

another spoon and offering it to him. He paused a moment, looking out to where his parents were, then turned back to join Raya at the island.

"Hey Dweeb," he said, taking a seat and grabbing the spoon she held up. "What are you eating here?"

"Mint Chocolate Chip," she said, scowling into the pint. "Broke up with my boyfriend, so I figured I might as well eat my weight in ice cream."

"I didn't even know you had a boyfriend," he said, giving her an empathetic frown.

"Yeah, well, now I don't, so there you go," she said with an impassive shrug.

He nodded, taking a big spoonful and pausing to ask, "Who was this guy? Anyone I know."

"Does it matter?" she countered.

"Not really, but I'm curious," he volleyed.

She rolled her eyes and took another large scoop onto her spoon. "Javier," she replied.

"Like, Rami's brother, Javier?" he screeched out, completely surprised by this new development.

Giving him an acknowledging nod, she turned her focus back to her ice cream, shrugging and let out a big sigh. "Yeah, well, it's over, so no need to get all protective brother on him."

Steve was about to reply and quickly closed his mouth. His sister was tough and always had been. There was no question, Raya could hold her own. He brushed his shoulder against hers and met her gaze. "If he needs an ass kicking let me know."

His comment elicited the shadow of a grin as he

clinked his spoon to hers and then scooped another big bite of ice cream.

The patio door slid open, his parents walking into the kitchen, interrupting their ice cream pity party. His mom was carrying a big basket of tomatoes, peppers, cucumbers, and lettuce from her garden and, as usual, had a bright smile to greet him.

"Hello, my sweet boy," his mother cooed as she came around and gave him a quick hug, balancing the almost overflowing basket in her hand. "Where's Em?" she asked curiously.

"She has an interview at the Arts Council this afternoon. One of their vocal teachers recently moved away, so they're urgently looking to replace her this fall."

"She would be perfect for that job," his father said, washing his hands at the sink and reaching for a dishtowel.

"I think so too," he replied with a smile as he added, "We've also been writing songs together and will be starting to record her first album soon. I've been learning more about production and have been using some of my connections to make it happen for her."

"Fantastic!" his dad replied, his smile wide. "Paying it forward."

"Yeah, she's very excited about it, and it will be my first project outside of the band."

"Expanding your horizons. Nothing wrong with that," his dad added.

His mom looked at him, eyes brimming with pride. "I'm really proud of you, Stevie. You've accomplished so many amazing things, and you have the biggest heart. When I think about where you and Raya came from, and at what incredible human beings you have both become..." she shook her head, and his father wrapped his arm around her supportively. "... I'm just grateful every day that I get to be your mom."

Steve glanced at his sister and nudged her shoulder, making her smile, and she replied with a roll of her eyes. "Yeah, yeah, we're awesome, we know!"

Laughter filled the room until all three of them looked towards Steve, knowing there was more to his visit than just catching up.

Steve caught their inquiring looks and chuckled. "Am I that obvious?"

All three nodded, and his father leaned onto the counter, his eyes twinkling with delight. "So, what's your plan for asking her?"

* * *

EMERSYN WALKED out of the Arts Council building, glowing like the sun and feeling like there was no way life could get any better. She had been hired on the spot for a job that would not only give her a chance to teach but didn't require her to go through years of university to start. She was replacing someone who had held this job for the past 15 years, and that realization gave her a peace of mind that this job had the potential for longevity. She strolled the five blocks to home, as it dawned on her that she could walk to work now too. *Could it get any better?*

She reached the big, beautiful grey house and walked up the stone steps to the front door, every time just as enamoured by this warm, welcoming home as she was the first time Steve brought her here.

"Oh, Emersyn, dear girl!" the sweet voice of Nonni sounded. "Do you have some time to sit and visit with an old woman?"

She looked at Steve's grandmother relaxing on the front porch in a wicker loveseat, a book on her lap, and a table with a pitcher of iced tea and a plate of cookies. It was like she was expecting her and had set out her own version of afternoon tea for them. Emersyn smiled, nodded, and turned to join her, taking a seat beside her on the loveseat.

"Help yourself." She said, gesturing to the spread before them.

Emersyn poured herself and Nonni a glass of iced tea and grabbed a cookie, nibbling it as she contentedly sat with her. "This is nice." Emersyn said, breathing in the scent of the remaining roses from the bushes that lined the deck.

"It is, isn't it?" Nonni replied. "I always like to sit out here on days like this. Not too hot, not too cold," she said in a musing tone. "Reminds me a little of Tom and me. Two opposites that make a perfect balance."

Emersyn took in her words as a smile tugged at her lips. "Sounds like Steve and I too."

Nonni turned her gaze to meet her eyes, her beautiful cherry lipstick smile, as usual, on pointe. "You and my sweet Stevie remind me of Tom and I when we were younger. We too were so different, fiery and passionate. Not always a bad thing." she said, giving her a gentle nudge and wiggling her perfectly penciled eyebrows. "A challenge at times, but what's life without a little challenge? Makes life more interesting." she declared, taking a sip of her iced tea and setting down the glass. "65 years of driving each other crazy, but I wouldn't trade it for anything." she said wistfully, meeting Emersyn's gaze. "Sometimes it's those challenges that help us to grow into the person we want to be."

Emersyn took in her words, feeling them deeply as she replied, "I hope Steve and I have as good a life as you and Nonno have had."

She patted her arm gently, her touch warm and comforting. "Oh, you will. If you love each other fiercely, you'll be right here years from now reminiscing about a life well lived."

* * *

WALKING UP THE SIDEWALK, Steve could hear Emersyn's unmistakable laugh, along with Nonni's bountiful voice. He approached the steps to the front deck and stopped listening as his grandmother continued with her story.

"Then my Tom, he decided that he was going to try to impress me. He jumped the curb with his old Cadillac, sideswiped a streetlight and broke the front wheel clean off. Men are so silly!"

"Men are what, Nonni?" Steve asked, climbing the stairs to find them huddled together on a wicker loveseat, like best friends, thick as thieves.

"I was just telling Emersyn, that you men are such idiots when you are in love! Honestly, complete buffoons!" Nonni proclaimed, her eyes dancing with mirth.

Emersyn gave him an amused look, her eyes glazed over with tears of laughter as she waited with bated breath for his response.

He smirked in defence as he replied, "I think we act like complete buffoons because we get blinded by your feminine wiles."

Nonni's cheeks rose, and a bright smile curved her cherry lips. "My wiles may be less wily these days, but I know a buffoon answer when I hear one." Nonni deadpanned, making them both laugh, and Steve shrugged as she winked at him playfully.

Nonni glanced between them and reached out for their hands, taking them in hers she said. "Now promise me one thing. That no matter how life challenges you and no matter how frustrated or angry you get with each other, you never forget how much you love each other. If you focus on that love, rather than the pitfalls, you'll be here just like me now on this porch in 50 years wondering where the time has gone."

Steve reached for Emersyn's other hand and met her eyes, flashes of their future running through his mind as he answered, "There's no place I'd rather be."

CHAPTER 15

"Absolutely beautiful job, Hailey. I will see you next week." Emersyn said to one of her voice students as she exited her classroom. Glancing at her watch, she reached for her jacket and purse and turned to lock her classroom door. Waving goodbye to a colleague, she slipped on her jacket and zipped it up as she noticed the wind blowing the fallen leaves across the parking lot. The October weather was getting colder, but she still loved her walk to work. Exiting the building, she passed the arts building and a few residential homes, passed the City Works building and crossed the bustling main street of St. Augustine to head down her street. *Her street.* She loved saying it. Since moving in with Steve two months ago, she couldn't help but feel a sense of peace and belonging. What was once her quiet, lonely life was now filled with friends, family, and music. Not only music through her new job, but their music. Music she and Steve had created. They had been writing like fiends and now had a dozen amazing songs that she was set to start recording this weekend, making a long-time dream come true.

Arriving in front of the big, beautiful character home she had fallen completely in love with, she took a moment to drink it in before she climbed the stone stairs to the porch. Unlocking the door, she stepped inside, shaking off any leaves that stowed away from her walk, and slipped off her jacket. She hesitated at the bottom of the stairs and listened for signs that Nonno and Nonni were home. The house was quiet. She adored spending time with them and cherished every bit of laughter and advice they shared as she looked forward to their endless stories.

Climbing the stairs, she unlocked their apartment door and stepped inside, turning to hang her jacket and slip off her shoes.

"Steve!" she called out, knowing he should be home.

She turned and her breath caught, her hand coming to her heart as she took in the spectacle before her. The entire open main space of their apartment was a sea of little candles and glowing light, illuminating the large space. Looking around, there was no sign of Steve, but she noticed a card sitting on the kitchen island. Picking it up, she saw her name was scrawled on the front in his handwriting, and when she opened it, the notecard inside read:

Follow the lights around the room and count all the ways I love you. There are 100, so be sure to count each one.

With wide eyes, she glanced around the room. On every possible surface stood a candle, each with what appeared to be a sticky note next to it. She walked to one on the table, #1 and picked up a heart-shaped sticky note. *I love Em's laugh, it's infectious.* She followed each numbered light, picking up sticky notes saying, *the cute way she curls up her nose when she's unsure of something, the way she wraps herself around me at night and sighs.* Each note, describing little things she possessed and things she did that he loved. She found the last candle labeled 100 and picked up the sticky note, which read, *Turn around.*

She whirled around and Steve stood in the middle of the room, holding up a heart note for her to see. She met his beautiful onyx gaze, her eyes shining with tears as she approached him slowly, making his handsome lips curl up into a grin.

"I have reason 100 right here," he said, holding up the sticky note. "Do you want to read it?" he asked, holding it just out of her reach.

"I do." She said, looking up at him through her long lashes.

Placing the note in her hand, she glanced down and read aloud:

"I love you, Em, and I can't imagine my life without you. Say yes and let's start this thing called forever."

She looked up at him, her eyes wide as she watched him drop to one knee and pull a ring out of his pocket, holding it out to her. "What do you say? Will you marry me?"

Emersyn blinked rapidly, tears blinding her vision as she looked down at the man she loved more than life itself. They had come so far in such a short amount of time, and yet it felt like he was always destined to be with her. Like fate played a hand in reuniting them and bringing them to this place, right now with him on one knee. Taking his handsome face in her hands, his eyes searching hers for the answer, she leaned in, brushing her lips to his, then pulled back only a breath away, her eyes locked on his as she answered. "Yes."

With eyes morphing from questioning to pure elation, he took her hand, slipped the diamond solitaire ring on her finger and stood, lifting her into his arms. She wrapped her legs around his waist, and he embraced her with passion, their kiss sealing their promise to each other.

A knock on the door broke them from their moment, and the door creaked open, his mother's blonde head peeking inside. "Are we able to come in now?" She asked, opening the door to reveal both of his parents, Raya, Nonno and Nonni. Behind them were Rami, Savanah, Layne, Juli, and Tabitha.

They all walked into the apartment and circled them, their faces curious and questioning. "So?" Raya asked with a laugh. "Don't leave us in suspense here. What did you say?"

Emersyn looked up at Steve and wiped the wetness on her cheeks with the heel of her hand. "I said yes!"

With that, they swarmed them with hugs, kisses, congratulations, and tears. All these people, who loved and supported them, showered them with love.

"Hey, you got room for one more?" a familiar husky voice asked from across the room. Everyone turned, and standing by the door was... Rex.

* * *

STEVE STOOD there staring at his best friend standing at the door of his apartment. He looked thinner, a little placid. There were a few visible scars on his face, but his familiar royal blue eyes shone with his apprehensive smile. Gone was his signature blue mohawk, replaced by a short brush cut in his natural brunette and a light dusting of stubble on his chin. Their loved ones parted, and Steve glanced down at Emersyn, her eyes urging him to go to his friend. He walked towards Rex, mounting emotion rising in his chest with each step forward. Rex tentatively walked towards him, and Steve looked down at oldest and dearest friend, tears in his eyes. Rex's gaze glazed over and mirroring his emotion.

Rex cleared his throat and put his hand out to Steve. "Congrats, man. You're going to be a fuckin' awesome husband." Steve let out a deep, rich laugh, took his offered hand, and pulled him in for a hug, rogue tears over-flowing onto his cheeks. Rami and Layne approached, joining in on the embrace, all the guys overcome with emotion and laughing between their tears. Rex would be okay. The band was back together, and nothing was going to tear them apart again.

The celebration lasted until the wee hours, all family had gone home, leaving only the band, their wives and a sleeping Tabitha curled up on Juli's lap.

"We're so glad you are back and okay." Savanah said, putting her hand on Rex's shoulder as she passed him a can of soda.

Rex gave her a grateful smile and glanced around the room at his bandmates. "I've missed you guys," he proclaimed as he looked down at his hands holding the soda. "I know I disappointed you, and I'm sorry about the album and the tour. Damn, I'm so fucking sorry about everything."

"You gave us quite a scare." Rami said, his wary eyes meeting Rex's. "We thought we'd lost you."

Rex pursed his lips and looked away, trying to tamp down the emotion that was threatening to spill again as he managed. "Truth is, I lost myself."

No one responded, his words hanging in the room like a noose. He had come so close to death and, by the grace of God, had come through on the other side. Broken, bruised, far from the clear, but he was here in front of them, and for that everyone in the room was grateful.

"You know, I'm glad you're back because I need a best man." Steve said with a smirk, breaking the silence. "You think you could do the job?"

"Fuck yeah, I can," Rex responded. "When's the wedding?"

Emersyn giggled and shrugged; their engagement was hours old, so of course nothing had been discussed. Steve's eyes locked on Emersyn; his gaze unwavering as he answered, "This next summer in the back garden, when the rose bushes are blooming."

Everyone looked at Steve and then to Emersyn, whose eyes hadn't left Steve's. Her lips curled up in a smile as she replied, "Sounds perfect to me."

* * *

THEIR BEDROOM WAS SILENT, the wee hours of morning quaking after a long night with friends. They lay together, their bodies intertwined, as Emersyn lifted her hand, the diamond catching just a glint of light peeking through the curtains and making it sparkle. She sighed, lacing her fingers with his and looking up into his dark eyes as she confessed. "I can't wait to be your wife." Steve lifted her hand to his mouth and kissed her ring, placing her hand over his heart. "Thank you for loving me, just as I am. You've made every dream I dared to wish for come true." Steve tipped her chin up, their lips a hair's breadth apart as she continued, "You've given me so much. Is there anything you want from me?"

His delicious lips curved up into a tender smile. "You. You are my dream, Em. That's it. Just you, by my side forever."

She threaded her hand through his hair as she bridged the gap between them and kissed the man she loved. A man who saw her as whole instead of broken. Who embraced each and every scar, accepting that they are part of who she is and loving her because of them.

Pulling away, she met his gaze, her entire beautiful and blinding future reflected in his onyx gaze as she replied, "By your side is the only place I want to be."

* * *

THE NEXT EIGHT months flew by. Emersyn's first album, Love Notes, was released and was garnering acclaim as her first single, "Our Song" hit the charts and was being touted as the wedding song of the season. Prairie Sound was able to release their second album that winter and were planning to reschedule their national tour for the upcoming fall pending Rex's recovery. Life, although busy, settled into a contented calm, which was just the way they liked it.

As another spring passed and summer finally arrived, Steve found himself at the end of an aisle on a beautiful July afternoon in the backyard of his family's home. Everyone they held dear gathered under the shade of the oak trees. The day was warm, blue skies a promise, fragrant, colorful rose bushes in full bloom as Steve stepped forward. Rex clapped him on the shoulder, and he turned to smile at his best friend as everyone rose to their feet. His eyes darted back, looking down the aisle as he saw her. *My Em.* Cascading in delicate lace, her sweetheart dress, molded to her curves with perfection and flared out at her feet. Everything about the vision of her in the gorgeous white dress was stunning, but what stood out was the woman wearing it. Gone was the woman who doubted herself, who thought she wasn't enough or undeserving of love, and in her place was a proud, strong woman who exuded immeasurable confidence. He had never seen anyone or anything more beautiful. She locked him in her mesmerizing midnight stare and slowly strolled down the aisle towards him. Reaching the end of the aisle, she handed her bouquet to Dee as he stepped forward to take her hand.

"Well, you look very handsome." She said, smoothing out the lapel of his suit as she looked up at him through her impossibly long lashes.

"You are breathtaking." He replied on an exhale as he reached out and caressed her cheek and leaned down about to kiss her.

The minister cleared his throat as he stood before them, and Steve pulled away quickly, making everyone laugh.

"Clearly, Steve and Emersyn are ready to get this show on the road and get on to the wedded bliss part of marriage. So, as per the couple's request, we're going to keep this ceremony short and sweet," he said with a wink. "Let's jump right into your vows."

He stepped back, and Steve let out an exhale, giving Emersyn an amused smile. "Em, you and I go way back. So far back that the first time I met you has become a core memory for me. I remember you stuck out your tongue at me and how I thought you looked like a Disney princess in one of the movies Raya made me watch."

"You liked them, admit it!" Raya shouted from where she sat, eliciting snickers from their guests.

"Yeah, I probably did," he replied with a chuckle and turned back to meet Emersyn's gaze. "I knew even back then; you were special. Then we were thrown together, an unexpected reunion and very quickly I knew I wanted to be near you. I wanted to simply revolve in an orbit around you and bask in the brightness that is your star. You, Em, are the brightest star in my sky. I promise to love you the way you deserve to be loved, never stop telling you how amazing you are, and I promise to never dim your light. I love you."

Emersyn pulled a handkerchief from the bodice of her dress and dabbed at the tears that started to trail down her face. She tucked it back in as Steve's gaze drifted to her cleavage, causing him to raise an eyebrow and his lips curl into a grin. She shook her head and let out a little laugh as she took his hands.

"Steve, I think it's no secret I wasn't too thrilled when Dee paired us together last year. I wasn't exactly the President of the Steve Furgallo Fan Club and, well, if I was being honest, I was a little jealous of you. You walked into every room quietly confident, seemingly without a care in the world, and at the time I felt like the weight of the world was on my shoulders. But then, very quickly you got to me. You found your way into my guarded heart and showed me what love really is. You have shown me that love is unconditional. You have shown me that love is selfless. And most importantly, you have shown me that I am worthy of it. And I promise to love you like that in return for the rest of our lives."

Steve blinked, a rogue tear escaping down his cheek. She reached up to swipe the tear with her thumb.

"Rings?"

Rex and Dee, who stood beside them, handed over the rings to the minister. He held his hand over the rings and said a short prayer, then handed one to Steve.

"I, Steven Furgallo, take you, Emersyn Bridger, to be my wife. I promise to remember that neither one of us is perfect but will strive to remind myself of the ways we are perfect for each other. With this ring, I thee wed," he said, meeting her eyes and sliding the diamond band on her finger.

The minister handed Emersyn a ring, and she locked her gaze on Steve. "I, Emersyn Bridger, take you, Steven Furgallo, to be my husband. I promise to remember that neither one of us is perfect but will strive to remind myself of the ways we are perfect for each other. With this ring, I thee wed," she vowed as she slipped a platinum band on his finger. Both grinning ear to ear, the minister stepped forward.

"By the power vested in me by the Church of God and the Province of Manitoba, I hereby pronounce you husband and wife. Steve, you may finally kiss your bride!"

Steve wrapped his arms around her waist and picked her up, lifting her off her feet, bringing her face level with his. "Hey there, wifey."

"Hey there, hubby." She replied, hooking her arms around his neck. "Are you going to kiss me or what?"

"Don't need to ask me twice," he replied as he captured her lips and kissed her with all the love in his heart and the promise to be her partner, faithfully by her side for the rest of their lives.

EPILOGUE

5 YEARS LATER

Some memories are just so sweet and special you want to relive them every day. That is what the past five years had felt like for Steve. A continuous stream of memories that latched on as core memories and became part of the evolution of who he was becoming.

Living life with Emersyn has been more than he thought it could be. In the five years since their wedding, they had enjoyed a surprisingly simple life despite Prairie Sound's continued popularity and fame. When not on tour, their days were spent on long walks, spending time with his family and their friends, and countless hours at his old upright piano, creating songs that soothed their souls.

The passion between them had not waned, and every night they found each other tangled together, satisfied, and satiated. Even after their daughter, Belle, was born three days shy of their second anniversary, and despite the tiredness that came with a crying baby and late-night feedings, they always reached for each other in the darkness.

The last five years had brought with them many changes. The first being her mother moving to a facility only two blocks from their home. Although with the worsening condition, it had become rare for her mother to recognize her, Emersyn was vigilant with her visits, and having her mother close gave her a peace of mind that brought a resigned calm to their lives.

There were changes in their living arrangements as well. Nonno passed away shortly after Belle was born, and they moved their family downstairs to help care for Nonni. Although she was 90, she was still spry, and the closeness Emersyn had with her warmed his heart. As for their upstairs apartment, Raya moved in, and now the house was one big open family home.

Steve paused on the keys a moment and smiled as he listened to the familiar chatter and laughter from the kitchen. Nonni was teaching Emersyn and Raya her secret family recipes when he heard the familiar pitter-patter of little feet on the hardwood floor coming towards him. He turned to see Belle, her black ringlets bouncing and her midnight eyes twinkling. He straddled the piano bench and put out his arms to his three-year-old daughter, whose sweet smile shone bright on her beautiful face.

"Hello, my pretty girl! Want to play the piano with Daddy?"

She nodded and ran towards him as he lifted her into the air, making the sweetest giggle escape. Hugging her tightly, he lifted his long leg over the piano bench and set her down next to him on the bench.

"Daddy, play my song," she said, looking up at him through her long lashes.

He smiled and kissed her on the head as he positioned his fingers on the keys and started to play the song that brought back so many memories, "Dream a Little Dream of Me".

His daughter watched as his fingers glided from note to note, and he could swear she was memorizing each movement, reminding him so much of himself when he was young. He finished the song, and she clapped her chubby little hands together, demanding, "Again," with a giggle.

"You heard her." Emersyn said from behind him, placing her hands on his shoulders.

"Have you ever noticed how Belle watches me play? I swear one day she's going to sit at this piano and play it herself," he mused.

"Oh, probably." Emersyn replied. "Music is in her blood."

"Do you think we should get her in some lessons this fall?"

"No, let's just let her be a kid, and if she wants to play, she'll play," she said, taking a seat beside Belle on the bench. "Besides, between the two of us, she will learn everything she needs to know."

He nodded and leaned over, planting a kiss on Emersyn's lips.

"No kissing, only playing." Belle announced, scrunching up her nose and furrowing her brows.

"Bossy like her mother." Steve chuckled as he gave Emersyn a wink eliciting a roll of her eyes.

"Well, get on with it." Emersyn gestured with a wave of her hand for him to start.

He shook his head and chuckled as he started to play, Emersyn singing along. Steve looked to his hands gliding over the ivories, glanced down at his beautiful daughter beaming beside him and as his eyes raised to meet the gaze of the woman he loved with his entire heart and soul, his chest filled with gratitude for memories like these and the lifetime of memories left to share.

* * *

Continue reading about the members of Prairie Sound in the next book, *On The Edge Of Forever.* Buy now!

ALSO BY TANYA RENEE

Primrose Series

Prairie Sky

Prairie Nights

Prairie Fire

Prairie Hearts

Prairie Sound

Prairie Rain

With The Band

Finding Direction

Love Notes

On The Edge Of Forever

MORE FROM SERENADE PUBLISHING

Songbird

By Sarah Williams

Brigadier Station Series

By Sarah Williams:

The Brothers of Brigadier Station

The Sky over Brigadier Station

The Legacies of Brigadier Station

Christmas at Brigadier Station

Heart of the Hinterland Series

By Sarah Williams:

The Dairy Farmer's Daughter

Their Perfect Blend

Beyond the Barre

The Outback Governess

By Sarah Williams

The Spring of Love Series

By Virginia Taylor

Forever Delighted

Forever Amused

Forever Heartfelt

The Tooth Fairy Chronicles

By Victoria Rocus

Tooth Decay With A Side Of Fae

Toothaches And Wedding Cakes

Baby Tooth And Tangled Roots

Wisdom Tooth And The Awful Truth

Toothpicks And Wicked Tricks

A New Page

by Aimee MacRae

It Happened in Paris

By Michelle Beesley

The Bondi Bubble

By Megan Krolik

For more information visit:

www.serenadepublishing.com

ACKNOWLEDGMENTS

Hello again happy readers! As always I have a lot of people, I want to thank them for making this enemy to lovers story come to life.

Firstly, I want to acknowledge my husband, Bart, for setting up one of my favorite scenes in this novel by insisting our family go hiking on one of the hottest days of the summer months. Yes, I admit it. I melted down on a hiking trail the tension not unlike the tension between Steve and Emersyn in said scene. Thank you for not letting me die on that trail and as always loving me just as I am, drama queen and all. You are my biggest champion. Love you Bear.

To my kids, Theo and Raina who are simply two of the funniest and coolest people I know. Pretty sure you got that from me. Wink, wink.

To my Mom and Dad, I can't thank you enough for all you've given me, not only as a kid growing up but as an adult. I am who I am because of your unconditional love.

To my readers, who continue to join me on this crazy ride. Thank you for getting so invested in the stories I write and for telling me how much you enjoy them. I love hearing your comments, reading your reviews and sharing your excitement as each new story releases. You've made this journey so much fun. I love you all!

To my exceedingly patient piano teacher, Lorna Dyck, who taught me for eight whole years despite my very obvious lack of talent. You never squashed my excitement and thirst for learning, and through your lessons you instilled in me some valuable lessons that I still carry with me today. Persistence and a never give up attitude. Thank you.

To the city I call home, Steinbach, Manitoba, and the inspiration of St. Augustine. Thank you for embracing my writing and celebrating it with me. I've received so much support from this community and am as always grateful.

And lastly, to Sarah Williams and the entire team behind her at Serenade Publishing. Thank you for giving me the opportunity to live this dream! Go Team Serenade!